NOWHERE LAND

Also by K.A. Applegate

ANIMORPHS®

REMNANTS™

NOWHERE LAND

K.A. APPLEGATE

AN
APPLE
PAPERBACK

SCHOLASTIC INC.
New York Toronto London Auckland Sydney
Mexico City New Delhi Hong Kong Buenos Aires

ISBN 0-590-88193-0

12 11 10 9 8 7 6 5 4 3 2 1   2 3 4 5 6 7/0

Printed in the U.S.A.
First Scholastic printing, January 2002

Dedicated to Michael
from me, from Michael to
me, from both of us to
Jake, and from
the three of us
to all of you.

(CHAPTER ONE)

"I'VE CROSSED THE EMPTINESS."

He had dreamed in the year 2011.

Five hundred years had passed since Billy Weir's dream. Five hundred years since he had dreamed of a loneliness so profound that no human had ever before experienced the like. Five hundred years since he had dreamed of the copper-colored sea and the huge, bouncing creatures and the sails, the white sails, and a grinning, wild-eyed kid hanging from the rigging and yelling at the top of his lungs.

A lot had happened since that dream.

The asteroid had destroyed Earth, broken it apart, obliterated all hope of human survival.

The *Mayflower* had departed only hours ahead of that catastrophic finale, carrying its hastily assembled human cargo.

Five hundred years since the still-experimental hibernation equipment had experienced failures that left some of the people shriveled and desiccated like mummies; caused others to sprout a persistent mold that ate the corpse; nurtured the growth of a mutated worm that tunneled through bodies, making Swiss cheese of loved ones.

For Billy Weir the failure had been different. The hibernation equipment had shut down his heart, lungs, kidneys. It had stopped cell division. For all intents and purposes, it had killed him — as it was designed to do. But where the others all lay unconscious, unaware of the worms, the mold, the dehydration, the impact of micrometeorites, unaware even of their own deaths, Billy Weir had remained awake.

For five centuries of silence he lay completely paralyzed, incapable of even the slightest movement, but awake, alert, aware of his own predicament.

In that time he had dredged through every memory in his own mind. He had even — so he believed, anyway — found a way to tap into the minds of his fellow human Remnants.

Certainly he had changed in some profound way. From this unique life he had acquired abilities no human had ever owned.

He looked no different, as far as he knew. He was

still slight, dark-haired, pale, with sunken dark eyes and a determined mouth. He was still the gloomy Chechnyan orphan who never quite became the sunny Texan his adopted parents hoped for.

Others had changed, too. Some didn't even know it, yet. But five centuries of radiation combined with the hibernation equipment's questionable reliability had caused mutations.

Or perhaps something else entirely had caused the mutations. Billy wasn't sure. During the long emptiness he had crossed and recrossed the line into madness. Sane, mad, normal, real, and unreal were all obsolete terms for Billy.

Billy had slowed down. Way down. When at last the *Mayflower* was captured by the impossibly vast ship the Blue Meanies called Mother and the survivors were revived, they seemed to Billy like buzzing flies. They flitted by at speeds so great he could hardly track them. They spoke in blurts of hyper-speech.

Billy knew things had changed. He knew he was off the *Mayflower*. He knew that Jobs and Mo'Steel had carried him on a stretcher for a long time. He remembered draining the life from his pain-wracked, worm-eaten adoptive father, Big Bill. He remembered the way he could transmit Jobs's speech to the Blue Meanie back in the Tower of Babel.

But Billy also remembered other things: growing vast golden wings and flying into the sun; seeing his fingers and toes become roots and branches of a tree that then withered and died; listening to his birth mother's voice telling him to rise up and destroy the invader.

He remembered things that may have happened, and things that probably did not. He no longer had any way to know which was which.

Billy Weir knew he was insane. But then how could a madman know he was mad?

He had dreamed of copper seas and vast, bouncing creatures as big as blimps. He had dreamed of tall masts with vast sails and Mo'Steel — yes, it had been Mo'Steel in the dream, he saw that now — shouting from the rigging, shouting at the wind.

I've crossed the emptiness, he told himself. *The circle is closing. Or maybe I'm still on the* Mayflower, *and none of this is real.*

And maybe it doesn't matter.

(CHAPTER TWO)

"ALL YOU NEED'S A SCREWDRIVER, DUCK. A SCREWDRIVER AND SOME DUCT TAPE."

"Jobs!"

2Face almost collapsed with relief. She'd hoped it was him, but in the gloomy light, and with only glimpses through the low, swirling fog, she couldn't be sure. Now the intelligent face, the distracted, slightly bulging brown eyes that gave Jobs the look of a person surprised in the middle of doing something else, the mess of blond hair were clearly visible.

"Hi, 2Face. Is Edward with you?"

2Face nodded. "Edward is fine."

"We saw Riders chasing you guys. I thought . . . it looked like they . . ."

"We're all still alive," 2Face said. She could have added more. "Still alive" didn't exactly bring Jobs up to date on what had happened. But not right now. There was just too much to tell.

Jobs waded slowly through chest-deep water. Just behind him, partly hidden from view, was Mo'-Steel. They were rarely far apart. 2Face knew they were best friends. Mo'Steel had dark eyes, hair, and complexion. His face was broad, eyes far apart. He was an altogether less serious-looking person than Jobs. He seemed to vibrate with energy, like he was bouncing even when he was standing still.

Jobs and Mo'Steel had something between them, a floating log maybe. And coming up behind Mo'-Steel were Violet Blake — Miss Blake, as she liked people to address her — and Olga Gonzalez, Mo'-Steel's mother.

"What's up, 2Face?" Mo'Steel asked cheekily, as though they'd all just run into one another at the mall.

"Nothing good," 2Face answered.

The log between Jobs and Mo'Steel was no log. It was a human being, a pale, skinny boy named Billy Weir. He was floating faceup, presumably alive. Or what passed for life in Billy's case.

2Face had the thought that it was a pity Billy hadn't been with her and the others earlier, back on the tower. When it had come time to feed a living sacrifice to the baby, he would have been a natural victim.

An unworthy thought, she knew. But then again, she'd been the baby's original designated victim, and she figured she had a right to try and live, whatever the cost to someone else.

It had been a bad time.

And things weren't much better now. The Remnants, both groups, were wading through a seemingly endless marsh. The water was as deep as seven or eight feet in places, as low as two feet elsewhere, but generally about chest-high.

Here and there were islands. The fog would part to reveal them for a moment, then whisk them away, a magician's cape. The islands were little more than sandbars clotted with drifting vegetation, clumps of reeds, and some bizarre trees that looked a little like skittish palm trees, overreacting to every hint of a breeze. The trees were always swaying wildly, inappropriately, drooping way over before springing back.

A small fire had been seen on one island. No doubt it was the Riders. If the Riders came after them now, not even Tamara and the baby would be able to save them. The Riders skimmed about on hoverboards. They were formidable enough on dry land. With the humans all wallowing in the thick, warm water, the two-headed Riders would be entirely in charge.

Jobs stopped. He kept a hand on Billy Weir's foot. They weren't carrying the boy, just guiding him. He was rigid, lying straight and flat and somehow riding too high in the water, as if he weren't a real person at all with a real person's mass, but an inflated doll of himself.

"What are you doing out here by yourself?" Jobs asked 2Face.

2Face raised the eyebrow on the unburned side of her face. "You want a wisecrack or the truth? The truth will take a while."

Jobs focused past her, taking in the huddle of humans perhaps fifty yards farther on.

"Is Edward with them?"

2Face shook her head. This would be interesting. "He's right here. Edward, quit playing around, say hi to your brother."

"Hi, Sebastian," a voice said.

Even knowing where she had left him, 2Face couldn't immediately make Edward out. He was a wispy little kid and short enough that only his head was above water.

2Face was gratified to see Jobs's blank stare.

Then the wide look of surprise when Edward moved and at last he could see his little brother.

"What is that, camouflage?" Jobs asked.

"I'm the Chameleon," Edward said proudly. "It's like a superhero."

"This is something you *do?*" Jobs asked.

Olga Gonzalez said, "A mutation? Like the baby?"

"I'm going to change my name," Edward said. "From now on everyone has to call me Chameleon."

"Don't be stupid, you're not changing your name to Chameleon," Jobs snapped.

"Why not?" Edward wailed, outraged. "You changed your name, *Sebastian*. If you can call yourself 'Jobs' I can call myself 'Chameleon.'"

"He's got a point there, Duck," Mo'Steel said to his friend.

"2Face's name used to be Essence," Edward said helpfully.

"How about if we don't do this right here and right now, standing up to our teeth in water?" Jobs said. "I got stabbed in the butt and it hurts. What's left of Violet's finger is still a mess. Mo's cut and all burned and —"

2Face saw him glance guiltily at her own half-melted face. She didn't have time for his pity. Her face had almost gotten her killed, and might still. No more time for pleasantries. 2Face had to ensure that Jobs and Mo'Steel and Olga and Violet were on her side.

"Things have gone bad with us," 2Face said in a low, hurried voice. "Yago is trying to divide us, make us fight amongst ourselves. He tried to set up me and Edward for being . . . for being different. Tamara and the baby . . ." She took a deep breath and glanced anxiously over her shoulder. "Tamara's the only one who can fight the Riders. The baby, it has some kind of power or something, it can make her almost invincible. I saw her kick butt on six Riders. But the baby . . . you think I'm crazy, don't you?"

Violet Blake laughed dryly. "We've just come from hell as conceived by Hieronymus Bosch. We escaped with the help of a Blue Meanie who blew himself up to shut down some kind of node that's part of a big computer he calls Mother. Maybe we should agree that none of us is crazy."

2Face frowned. As crazy as her own story sounded, theirs sounded crazier. Maybe they were all crazy.

"2Face stabbed these two monsters with a spear," Edward said. "They were hurting me."

Jobs looked sharply at 2Face and nodded in

recognition. 2Face was relieved that Edward had brought it up. She had saved Edward's life. She wanted Jobs to feel obligated.

"The baby demanded food. Human food. Meat," 2Face said quietly.

"What?"

"Yago wanted to sacrifice me. I . . . I convinced him otherwise." How much should she tell? The truth? All of it? Or a lie that was close to the truth? "He changed his mind and decided to make it Wylson."

"Okay, slow down here," Olga said. She gave a little, nervous laugh. "You sound like you're talking about the baby consuming someone. A person."

"It almost did." 2Face nodded. "It almost ate your mom, Miss Blake. But then the whole tower just disappeared and we were falling through the air and landed here in the Dismal Swamp."

"How is my mom?" Violet asked, showing no readable emotion.

"I think she's okay. But I think maybe she got the idea I was responsible. You know, since it was supposed to be me, and it ended up being her," 2Face said in a rush. Then, to keep them from asking questions, questions that might uncover the fact that 2Face had set up Wylson, had in fact delivered the treacherous blow that had felled Wylson Lefkowitz-Blake and left her helpless before the baby, she asked her own question.

"What's this about a Blue Meanie?"

"His name was Four Sacred Streams," Mo'Steel answered solemnly. "He destroyed the node, which is the only reason any of us is alive right now."

"And what's this about his mother?"

"Not *his* mother. Mother." Jobs waved his arm around. "All of this is Mother. This ship, inside and out, is Mother. All of it operated by a computer that hasn't had so much as a scan in probably thousands of years. Mother is a computer. A messed-up computer that's been loaded with all the cultural and historical data we brought on the *Mayflower*."

2Face felt the strangest flicker of hope. "You're some kind of big computer genius, right, Jobs? That's your thing, right? You're a hard-core techie."

"If it runs on electricity, my boy Jobs can fix it," Mo'Steel said proudly.

Jobs snorted dismissively. "Yeah, I'm a real techie genius. Just one thing: Mother is about a million years more advanced. It's almost certainly some sort of quantum computer, with some unimaginable number of Qu-bits. Me fixing it's like some caveman who is real good at making stone wheels suddenly deciding he knows how to fix a car."

"All you need's a screwdriver, Duck," Mo'Steel said, and laughed. "A screwdriver and some duct tape. Fix Mother right up. That's what we do."

(CHAPTER THREE)

"THE SUN RISES, AND WITH IT, HOPE."

Yago saw them coming: Jobs, his creepy mutant brother, his monkey-boy pal, Mo'Steel's mother, the lovely and definitely time-worthy Miss Blake, Billy Weird, and, of course, 2Face.

What to do now? That was the question. What to do, and who to do it to.

How to play it? Like he and 2Face were allies? Or should he try to switch back to Wylson? And what about his two toadies, D-Caf and Anamull?

Hard to know how it was all going to play out.

Mostly, Yago realized, he was wet.

"This is so weird," D-Caf said.

"You think?" Yago said with nasty sarcasm.

"The sun is coming up," D-Caf offered helpfully.

"Yes. The sun rises, and with it hope. Hope for a better world. Hope for peace and love and uncomplicated happiness."

"Really?" D-Caf asked.

Yago glared at him. "Are you the dumbest human being left alive? We're up to our armpits in water. We're lost and probably surrounded by Riders. We have a leader who thinks she's running a business seminar and our only fighter is an alien baby who likes *meat*. We have no food, no weapons. . . ."

D-Caf grinned and raised something from below the surface of the water. "I have a weapon. Do you want it?"

Yago stared. A Rider boomerang. It was a cruel-looking thing, toothed blades all along one edge.

"When everything was dissolving and right before we fell, I picked it up," D-Caf explained.

"Give it here," Yago said, but without any great pleasure. He wasn't a weapons person. He had no clue how to throw the thing. In fact, it seemed likely he'd end up cutting off a few of his own fingers.

On the other hand, it was probably a good thing to —

"Aaahhh! Aaaahhhh!"

A cry of shrill panic.

Yago's head snapped around, looking for the cause. It was Roger Dodger, a kid, going wild, slapping at the water and looking like he wanted to jump up out of it.

The kid went still. He said, "I . . . I felt some-thing."

"You nearly gave me a stroke!" Burroway snapped.

"Maybe it wasn't anything," Roger Dodger said doubtfully.

Then Burroway shrieked. "Something bit me! It's in the water, something in the water bit me."

There was a pause, everyone waiting, staring, all conversation done for now. And then it was Shy Hwang yelping and holding up a bloody arm with something still attached, something squirmy and muscular. Panic took hold and everyone was run-ning, Yago included, running through the water, an absurd slo-mo parody of actual running.

At first the herd of people had no direction; it darted and circled like a flock of startled birds, then headed toward the nearest of the low islands.

Hwang kept shouting, complaining, yelling, though Yago could see that whatever had grabbed his arm had let go now.

"My leg!" someone screamed.

Yago splashed, digging his arms in to propel him-self forward, taking giant moon-gravity steps. His leading foot landed on nothing and he plunged face-down into the water. He sank beneath the surface.

Claustrophobia shot syringes of adrenaline into his bloodstream and his brain began to slip gears, catching, slipping again.

No air, no air, no air. His eyes were open, blind, nothing but brown silt, swirling mud choking him.

Then he felt it, the slide of flesh over flesh, the slimy touch of it across his belly. He slashed with the boomerang and came within an inch of gutting himself.

Yago screamed into the water and kicked against nothing.

Something grabbed his arm and pulled. He broke the surface, gasped, and tried to shake loose D-Caf's grip.

"Let go of me, you moron!" he yelled. He lowered his legs and touched ground. The water was up to his chest, no more.

"You were kind of splashing a lot," D-Caf said, giving him a sideways look. He held up the boomerang. "I got this back. You must have dropped it."

"One of those things attacked me," Yago said.

D-Caf held out the boomerang, ready to surrender it again.

"Keep it," Yago said. No way could he act as if the blade meant something. No way could he put himself any more in D-Caf's debt.

Rather than risk hitting another hole, Yago leaned into a swim. He was a strong swimmer, though only on the surface — not underwater — and he was soon well ahead of D-Caf.

The little twitch had seen him panic. Okay, everyone was panicking, but D-Caf had been calm and he'd seen that Yago was not. That was bad. No one could know about the claustrophobia. It was a glaring weakness. Someone would use it. Maybe even D-Caf himself. He was a twitch, but he was also the one who'd shot one of the *Mayflower* pilots. If you'd do that, you'd lock someone in a box without a second thought, lock them in a closet with no light and no handle on the door, bury them alive in a casket and . . .

"Get a grip, Yago," he told himself. "Get a grip. You're Yago. You're *Yago*, man."

Yago went through his ego mantra: Yago was the First Son. Son of the first African-American female President. He held undisputed title to "hottest teen" in America. The world. Everyone loved him, or else feared him. How many letters from how many girls? Hundreds of thousands. Millions. I want a picture, a lock of hair, a worn T-shirt, to see you, kiss you.

He'd been on the cover of just about every magazine. *TeenPeople* had named him "Sexiest Teen Alive." The *New York Times Magazine* had called him the "Brat-in-Chief." When he'd changed his hair to spring green, half the kids in the country had followed suit. When he'd had the cat-DNA eye treatment, it had suddenly become one of the most common cosmetic procedures.

He was Yago, after all. Even here, even with no White House, no magazines, no fans, no letters, no . . . he was still Yago.

The mantra calmed him. The claustrophobia terror had replaced the fear of whatever was in the water. And now, with the suffocation fear receding, he could see the other fear more objectively. The herd was still in full flight, wallowing heavily toward the island. Jobs and his little gaggle were vectoring in, too, the fear having proven contagious.

Yago slowed his pace. You didn't want to be the last person out of the water but, he sensed, you also didn't want to be the first person to step on that island.

He bobbed high, looking for Tamara Hoyle. She was moving at a leisurely pace, carrying the baby up on one shoulder. She wasn't worried about whatever was in the water. And she was in no hurry to reach the island. In fact, she was slowing down.

Yago stopped dead. He tread water till he realized he was now in shallows, less than waist high.

Yago's instinct for survival was ringing a big, loud bell. Tamara knew something. He didn't know how, but she knew something more than any of the rest of them did. Her and that mutant, eyeless freak of a baby.

He was a hundred feet from the island's edge. The sun was coming up behind it but the mist still seeped through the strange trees and alternately revealed and concealed it.

Wylson, Burroway, and Tate reached the island at about the same moment. They climbed soggily up onto the shore and immediately came the earsplitting metallic shriek of a Rider.

Two of the alien monsters appeared, stomping on foot through the mist. They stood there, staring balefully down at the humans with their faces full of insect eyes.

Wylson raised her hands as if in surrender. "We don't want to fight, we don't want to fight," she practically sobbed.

The humans still in the water froze. Even Tamara

was stock-still, waiting, watching. She seemed to feel Yago's eyes on her and turned to glare at him.

Suddenly, a sharp pain on the back of his thigh. He flailed, reached around, and touched something slime-coated and powerful.

It had him.

(CHAPTER FOUR)

"THE UNHUMAN LIVES."

Chirismontak Hadad-Chirismon, Warrior of the Vanascom Clan, Acolyte of the Unseen Star God, had fought the human-not-human and survived. Others had not. This was destiny. The Gods chose some to burn in the fire, chose others to drown or behead or feed to the worms or invert.

Death came from the Gods and was many-form and beautiful. Rebirth was a birth into a new death, and each new death would bring greater pain until the end, when the cleansed and renewed warrior would become one of the Sanctified Ancestors.

Chirismontak had gone into the battle with the human-not-human expecting death. The human-not-human creature, the Unhuman as some were calling her, the dark-skinned female who drew her power from the smaller Unhuman, had already defeated great warriors. Chirismontak had known only two deaths himself. He was no great warrior, not compared to warriors who had already died a dozen deaths.

Greater warriors had been killed by the Unhuman, to their great honor. Chirismontak had been spared by the sudden collapse of Mother's artificial environment.

They had all fallen through the air. The mounts couldn't fly so high, of course, but the fall had not been far. The surviving battle-partners had repaired to their lands to dismount and reflect.

It was puzzling. The Clan had attacked the human invaders, knowing them to be the cause of Mother's betrayal. Mother had changed the world for the benefit of these interlopers. So had warned the heralds of the Bonilivak Clan who had first met the human creatures. The herald Sincomantak Hadad-Sincoman had the first human kill. He had said the humans were slow and weak. And yet Mother had remade the world for them. Mother was a Great God, but the Gods were to be feared, not obeyed. A warrior stood strong against the Gods when the Gods turned against the Clan.

In the Clan Council there had been agreement: Destroy the humans and Mother would restore the world as it should be, the world of the Riders. But they had not destroyed the humans and yet Mother had restored the world.

It was a mystery.

And now the humans, including the Unhuman and the smaller Unhuman, were wallowing in the water, unable to float, with no mounts to ride.

"They seemed defeated," Chirismontak said to his battle-partner, Demscatilintak Hadad-Demscaltilint.

"The Unhumans live," Demscatilintak said. "The humans live. And yet, the world is restored."

"Mother has given us back our world."

"In Clan Council we said that Mother would not relent until the humans were destroyed. And yet, Mother has given us back our world."

"It is troubling," Chirismontak agreed.

Mother had surrendered, and the thought stuck hard in Chirismontak's mind that the victory had been no victory, that the Clan's courage had been . . . irrelevant.

"Victory comes from courage and death," Demscatilintak said. "What courage? What death?"

"This was a victory granted from some other cause."

The humans sloshed closer. They were speaking

now in their barbaric, grunting, and slithering tones. The Unhuman was there, plain to see through the mist. The power radiated from her, from the baby. It was a halo of red and green. A bright red arc connected the two of them. Much brighter than the dull lights that waxed and waned around the other humans.

But now Chirismontak saw a different light. One of the humans was floating at rest, it seemed, silent. Around him a halo of pale blue. A single color.

"Tell me what your God Eye sees, Demscatilintak."

Demscatilintak peered closer, then he looked back at his companion. "My God Eye sees what cannot be."

"We must tell the Council. A single-hued halo from that human. Maybe one of the great warriors can . . ." Chirismontak couldn't complete the thought: He knew that not even one of the manydeaths would have seen such a thing.

"They approach. They hurry. Are they attacking? Should we kill them?"

Chirismontak's eating head snapped greedily, but his soul felt troubled. His board, at rest, leaning against a tree, hummed in response to his distress.

He and Demscatilintak could attack the Unhuman now and kill her. The water would hinder her movements. The humans were rushing but were still very slowly going through the water. They were vulnerable.

Maybe.

But how could a good battle come from a troubled soul?

"See: They have a fish."

(CHAPTER FIVE)

"IF WE HAD A ROPE . . ."

"Ah! Help! Someone help!" Yago screamed.

Yago twisted, twirled crazily, as absurd as a dog chasing its tail.

D-Caf watched, amazed. There was nothing he could do. If he tried to help, then Yago would yell at him.

D-Caf looked past Yago and saw that the two Riders were watching, too, staring. Watching and beginning to tremble. The bifurcated legs were wobbling; seams that joined the two halves of their beetle carapace creaked. The teeth-gnashing mouth/head even stopped gnashing.

"They're laughing," D-Caf realized with sudden insight. The Riders were laughing as Yago did his mad dance.

The baby joined in with a high-pitched squeal and Tamara grinned reluctantly. Her grin was for the

Riders. She came striding over, shaking her head ruefully.

Tamara grabbed Yago by the neck with one hand and bent him forward across her bent knee. This shoved him facedown in the water and the reaction was instantaneous: He slapped the water with his hands and tried to kick.

Tamara grabbed the gray thing attached to Yago's thigh. It was two feet long, a sort of eel, D-Caf supposed. Like an eel with an oversized sucker mouth.

Tamara gave the eel a practiced twist and it came loose with a wet, sucking *pop*. She released a spluttering, cursing Yago. She gave a slight nod toward the two Riders and then heaved the eel through the air.

The eel looked as though it would land in the mud. At the last second one of the Riders snatched it out of the air with one four-fingered hand, ripped the slimy thing in half, handed one piece to his companion, and tossed the rest into his own mouth.

The mouth/head chomped sloppily, noisily, as the main head stared impassively. The mouth/head then disgorged a tangle of clean bones.

"If I were you, I'd get off their island," Tamara said.

Wylson, Burroway, and Tate all complied instantly.

The two Riders watched as the humans began to move away.

D-Caf wasn't sure if he should catch up to Yago or not. Yago was touchy, probably on account of his claustrophobia. Yago thought no one knew, but D-Caf had noticed it before. D-Caf noticed a lot of things other people missed. For one thing, he had known Edward was becoming some kind of chameleon long before anyone else noticed.

D-Caf had been raised by his brother, Mark. Their parents had died and Mark had managed to maintain the household by himself through deception and manipulation. D-Caf would always be grateful to Mark for that, for not being sent away to live with relatives or even to end up in foster care.

But Mark had his problems. And D-Caf had learned to get along with his mercurial, amoral older brother. And now, Yago. Not so different from Mark.

D-Caf knew how to take abuse. And he knew how to keep his focus on the big picture. Yago was not his brother, or even his friend, but Yago needed him in a way, and no one else did. No one else would ever look past the killing — the panicked, accidental killing — of that shuttle pilot.

The group sloshed away from the island, wandered on without a goal, then, as individuals began to stop, the group came to a halt, centered around Wylson.

D-Caf was surprised by this. He knew that Yago had betrayed Wylson. He and Anamull both were present when 2Face made the case for trading her own life for Wylson's. Yet the group still gravitated to Wylson as leader, not to Yago.

D-Caf waded closer, instinctively moving toward Yago and Anamull. He watched Wylson closely. He had both her and her daughter, Miss Violet Blake, in the same frame. Once Wylson had looked much harder than her daughter. But now that difference was gone, almost reversed. Wylson had scared eyes now. She was uncertain. Insecure. She glared suspiciously at Yago. But interestingly, she seemed to be ignoring 2Face. She didn't know, D-Caf realized. She didn't know that 2Face had hit her from behind.

Miss Blake still wore the lace and frills of a "Jane," but the effect was completely ruined now. Her pale hair hung long and wet, with strands plastered on her cheeks. The dress was tatters and shreds. Everyone's clothes looked bad, but there was something especially noticeable in the decay of such a feminine garment.

The Jane's visible restraint, the deliberately portrayed self-possession, and the don't-touch-me aura were mostly gone. Violet Blake had lost a finger, nothing left but a filthy red bandage. She had also lost most of her reticent mannerisms. She was thin and tall, and before she had looked like someone who could snap in two or at least faint. She was still thin and tall, maybe thinner, like all of them had become, but now she definitely didn't look like she'd faint.

Maybe it was the pain, D-Caf thought. Maybe the pain from her hand had changed her. Or else what she'd seen and done since waking to the nightmare of this world.

Have I changed like that? D-Caf wondered. He didn't think so. He still felt awkward and inappropriate. Yago called him "Twitch."

Why haven't I changed like that? he wondered.

"We have to find some dry land," Burroway said. "The water's warm, but the human body can't survive half-submerged forever. We need dry land."

D-Caf thought of a joke. "At least now we can pee without having to go and . . ."

The joke was not welcome. Burroway, the

cranky old professor of whatever, looked as if he'd like to strangle D-Caf.

"See?" D-Caf told himself. "Inappropriate."

"We should pick a direction, fan out, keep moving, and search for dry land without Riders," Yago said forcefully.

It sounded good to D-Caf.

"Shut up," Wylson snapped at Yago. Her teeth were actually bared. Like a dangerous animal. Yago recoiled.

Wylson stepped closer to Yago. "You don't think I know what you did? You hit me from behind. You knocked me out. You don't think I know, you manipulative little monster?"

Yago didn't take another step back. He stood his ground now. "You're paranoid, Wylson."

"You tried to feed me to the baby!"

Yago laughed. "What, are you nuts? You were trying to feed 2Face to the baby. Don't you remember? The fall must have scrambled your brain. You told me to grab 2Face and I said you had to do it yourself, and when you tried, 2Face nailed you."

"Liar!" Wylson said, but without as much conviction as might be expected.

Yago sensed it, too, and shook his head sadly.

"You were sacrificing 2Face and ended up almost getting sacrificed yourself. So don't go all outraged on us, Wylson."

Wylson's gaze flickered over to 2Face, who stared stonily.

D-Caf knew he'd made the right choice: Wylson was smart, but Yago was more ruthless and determined. D-Caf needed a protector, and only Yago would do.

"I saw it," D-Caf said, speaking up despite worry about yet again saying the wrong thing. "It was just like Yago said."

Wylson frowned. She wasn't sure. Yago was impassive. And D-Caf felt a rush of pleasure: He'd said the right thing. Yago would be pleased.

Violet Blake said, "I have an idea: How about if no one eats anyone? I can't believe you, Mother. You're sickening."

"It was the baby," Wylson said, seeming to collapse into herself. "Tamara and the baby. We had no choice. The Riders . . ."

"I think we should focus on what to do now," Olga Gonzalez said quietly, scarcely concealing her disgust.

Her son, Mo'Steel, pointed. "What's that?"

"The sun coming up," Tate answered. "Or whatever they have for a sun here."

"No. No. Something moving." Mo'Steel shaded his eyes. "Like a . . . like a hippopotamus or something. Jobs, man, up on my shoulders."

Jobs climbed onto his friend's shoulders, the better to see. "Hey, it is moving. More than one. Like . . . like blimps or something. Maybe coming this way. I can't tell how far away they are because I don't know the scale."

Jobs slid back down into the water. In response to all the silent stares he shrugged. "I don't know what they are."

Wylson tried to regain control of the situation and formulate a plan, but all the focus was on the Blimps now. The sun was up, the sea was taking on the color of a new penny, and the Blimps were coming closer, ever closer, and could be clearly seen.

"Maybe we can hitch a ride on . . . whatever they are. If we had a rope . . ." 2Face said.

"Lasso it?" Jobs asked. "They're the size of blue whales."

"Pitons," Mo'Steel said. "You can't rope it, but if you had something sharp, a rock-climbing rig or, you know, spikes, or . . ." He shrugged.

"How about one of those Rider boomerangs?" D-Caf suggested.

Yago rounded on him, furious. In a flash D-Caf had undone all his good work with Yago.

"Okay, give it to him," Yago snarled.

(CHAPTER SIX)

"I THINK THIS IS OUR BUS."

Mo'Steel knew he shouldn't be happy. It was wrong. Clearly wrong.

But, man, whatever else negative you could say about Mother's world, there were some omnipotent rushes to be had here. He was playing matador to bulls the size of cruise ships.

They were cool creatures, the Blimps. One had come bouncing past, too far off to reach. They were a hundred feet tall and twice that in length and yet they bounced as lightly as balloons. Clearly they were filled with air or gas or something other than flesh and blood, because nothing that big and solid could do anything but sink and squash.

They had a few hundred very short legs, like cilia, under the back third of their bodies. The creepy thing was that the cilia were about the size and about the color of a Caucasian human leg, so they looked like someone had attached a hundred amputated limbs onto the bottom of the Blimp. These motored wildly, undulating in sequence. Each time the Blimp touched down, the cilia would hit the water and paddle the beast into its next forward bound.

If the vast, salmon-colored animals had any other external feature, Mo'Steel had not seen it. No eyes, ears, tails, or arms.

"Here comes one," Jobs said. "I think it'll come close."

Mo'Steel squinted. The sun was pretty bright now, at least by contrast with the last few days. And the copper sea reflected it in blinding flashes.

"I don't know, Duck. I'm thinking he's too far to the right. But some of them have to come close."

The Blimp herd's size was hard to guess: They blocked one another from view. Mo'Steel had counted at least seven, but that might be all. Or there might be five hundred more coming right behind them.

Mo'Steel had taken the boomerang and with Jobs's help knotted and weaved together belts and shirtsleeves and underwear elastic to make a ten-foot rope of sorts. The boomerang was attached to the rope at one end, and the other end was looped around Mo'Steel's left wrist. Ten feet wasn't much: The Blimp would have to come close.

Twenty minutes passed till he was able to take his first shot. The boomerang hit, stuck, then tore loose, and the Blimp was past. Impossible to chase the creature in the water. The Blimps were moving at only about five miles per hour, but that was faster than even Mo'Steel could run through chest-high water.

Then, just as he was about to make his second attempt, he was struck by an eel that glommed onto his knee and made him miss his chance.

An hour passed. And another. And now it was clear that the herd was mostly gone. Just a handful of the behemoths were still on approach.

Mo'Steel tried to ignore the rising chorus of complaints, advice, and bitter accusations that wafted toward him from the group. They were sick of standing helpless in the water. They were hungry — although no one at least was thirsty after they broke down and decided to sample the copper-colored water.

More than hungry and bored, the Remnants seemed to Mo'Steel to be dispirited. A fistfight actually broke out between Burroway and T.R., but the water kept them from doing too much damage to each other. A three-way shouting match involving Wylson, Yago, and 2Face came shortly thereafter.

Mo'Steel made a disgusted noise.

"We're not an impressive bunch of people, are we?" Jobs commented as they watched another Blimp float past, well out of reach.

"I don't know, 'migo," Mo'Steel said. "I guess everyone's pretty shook up, is all."

"This should be the cream of the crop. I mean, look who we have: a bunch of people who were either brilliant or successful or else the children of people who were brilliant or successful. Burroway and T.R. slapping each other?" Jobs shook his head.

Mo'Steel had to smile. Somehow anytime Jobs grew depressed or morbid it always shook Mo'Steel out of his own bad mood. "Having a Ph.D. isn't quite the same as being a saint."

"No. I guess not. But, man, we're it. We're all that's left of *Homo sapiens*. We have a responsibility not to be complete sphincters."

Mo'Steel laughed. "Sphincters?"

"Hey, my butt hurts, all right? I got stabbed in the rear, remember? Who knows what this water is doing to it. Probably a thousand alien germs and viruses. So, sorry if my mind is on the butt area, in general."

Mo'Steel squinted. Definitely a Blimp on track. Ten minutes away still. "My mom says probably not. The germs, I mean. She is a biologist. So . . ."

Jobs shrugged. "Yeah, probably not. This is Mother's default setting, but why would she stock the program with viruses? Let alone viruses that feed on humans? Come to think of it, we're the virus in this environment."

"It's kind of pretty, though, isn't it?" Mo'Steel said. "I mean, if we weren't standing in it, but we were on a boat just looking at it? The water and the weird shaky trees and the Blimps and all?"

Jobs gave him a sour look. "Sometimes you just get on my nerves, you know that?"

But Mo'Steel knew he'd pushed one of Jobs's buttons: The boy was a sucker for beauty. A well-formed tree, a sunset, a suddenly revealed panorama, they could freeze Jobs in midword, make him forget what he was doing, leave him staring, silent, oblivious to anything else.

And that's what he was doing right now. Mo'-Steel heard the silence. Jobs was taking it all in, getting around the fact that he was in a mess and appreciating the beauty of the mess.

Mo'Steel returned his own attention to the Blimp. It was coming straight on. Maybe a little left. Yeah, a little left.

"I think this is our bus," Mo'Steel said.

Jobs gave a startled jerk, focused, nodded. "Oh. Yeah. Looks good."

Mo'Steel began drifting left. Then he started running, slo-mo steps through the water, thrashing and splashing as the Blimp closed in.

"Get it this time, get it!" someone shouted.

"Go, Mo! Go, Mo!"

Mo'Steel shot anxious looks over his shoulder, ran, plunged into a hole, and went under. He came shooting right back up but now had to swim to catch the Blimp, and swimming with ten feet of rope and a boomerang was not easy.

His feet touched down, and now the water was only thigh-deep. He ran in great, splashing bounds as the gigantic balloon loomed over him. It was huge, an impossibly vast volume, yet not frightening. Mo'-Steel was a tick trying to hitch a ride on a passing Great Dane.

He would get his shot, he realized. He would get his shot.

He stopped, poised, took a steadying breath, and threw the boomerang.

It hit and slid off.

"You idiot!" someone shouted, probably Yago.

Frantically Mo'Steel reeled in the rope, cut his hand on the boomerang, ignored the blood, felt an eel suddenly hit his calf, ignored it, ran straight at the wall of salmon flesh, and rather than throwing the boomerang, reached as high as he could and slammed it hard into the skin.

The barbs of the boomerang blade held, the rope yanked in his hands, and all at once he was being dragged through the water.

He coiled up, drew his feet forward, and extended them. Too slow for real water-skiing, but maybe he could gain a sort of foothold on the water itself.

He wrapped the rope around one wrist again and dug his free hand into the flabby skin of the Blimp. It gave way, poked inward, almost without resistance.

Mo'Steel pulled his hand back out, frowned, considered as he passed the others at jogging speed. He spread his fingers wide and kneaded the flesh, gathered it, and yes, was able to grab a handful.

"Ha," he said.

He repeated the move with his other hand and now he had two flabby handfuls of the Blimp. He released and grabbed and pulled himself up. And again, released and grabbed and pulled himself up.

He climbed slowly, slowly past where the boomerang stuck. Up till his feet were out of the water.

The Blimp was turning ponderously away from the boomerang.

Mo'Steel took a chance and yanked the boomerang out, holding on by nothing but a handful of loose skin. He reached up high and slammed the boomerang back in. Using the rope and the flab-grab technique, he pulled himself up till he was a dozen feet above the water.

And now the physiology of the Blimp was working in his favor. The Blimp's mass spread out at the bottom. This resulted in a bulge that was nearly vertical for about ten feet but that then began to slope gently inward.

Mo'Steel actually felt himself sinking a little, like he was facedown on a soft bed. His whole body now formed a seal with the Blimp and he no longer worried much about sliding off.

He rested, arms spread wide, breathed, and considered. He was on the Blimp. Now what? How to get the others up?

The rope's end dangled just a foot or two above

the water, but the Blimp was well past the ma-
rooned humans. Past, but coming slowly around.
The boomerang was turning the Blimp, like a spur in
a horse. The Blimp was trying to move away from
the source of discomfort.

"You can be steered, huh?" Mo'Steel asked the
beast.

Maybe. Maybe it could be steered. But it would
be like trying to steer an oil tanker. The Blimp was
not fast or nimble.

Mo'Steel left the rope hanging and resumed his
ascent. He would need to use something else to
cause the massive beast some motivating pain. And
he didn't have much to work with.

(CHAPTER SEVEN)

"MAYBE THEY'RE BUFFALO."

"Is he biting it? Is he biting the Blimp?" D-Caf asked.

Jobs shielded his eyes and squinted. Mo'Steel could be seen quite clearly atop the Blimp as it circled slowly, slowly back. His friend was bent over, seemingly digging his face into the Blimp's flesh and shaking it like a terrier with a rat.

"I think he's biting the Blimp," Jobs admitted. In the back of his mind was the suspicion that this was just some kind of weird rush for Mo'Steel. Though he was hard put to figure out why biting the animal — if that's what it was — would be much of a thrill.

The Blimp was coming around slowly and Wylson had organized everyone to be ready. They were going in what she described as "reverse life raft" order: The strongest would go first to help the weaker coming behind.

That had led to some disagreements and hurt feelings, but Tamara and the baby were first in line, followed by Anamull with T.R., and then Yago. The rest were parsed out in a long line with hundred-foot intervals. Jobs was at the tail end, playing tugboat to the floating Billy Weir. He was about a quarter mile from where Tamara waited, and he had absolutely no idea how he was ever going to get Billy up the side of the Blimp.

The Blimp bounded closer now, definitely in line to intercept the Remnants. Mo'Steel was racing in big trampoline steps from one side of the creature to the other, pausing to stare, measure, then bend over and savagely bite the flanks of the behemoth.

"He's steering it," 2Face said.

"It's funny," Edward said and laughed.

The three of them, along with Violet and D-Caf, were the tail end of the line. They had moved a little closer for sociability. The Blimp was bouncing along in line now and Mo'Steel leaned out over the side and yelled something Jobs couldn't hear.

Tamara slung the baby onto her back, snatched the rope, and all but ran up the side of the Blimp and then, ignoring everyone else, she used the altitude to take a good look around.

Anamull grabbed the rope and pulled himself up

quickly and easily. He then lay flat against the Blimp and stood by as T.R. grabbed and hauled.

Mo'Steel, Anamull, and T.R. flattened themselves against the Blimp, each holding handfuls of skin, leaning in to create depressions. Yago joined them and now, as the subsequent passengers boarded, they were passed roughly up along this human chain.

Burroway missed his grab. So did Wylson and Tate and Violet.

2Face and Edward both succeeded in boarding.

Jobs waited, poised, with Billy Weir floating like a log. He was in shallow water, so he could at least give Billy a good heave-ho.

Mo'Steel slid down the rope, wrapped it around his arm, and extended a hand.

"We'll have to come back around for you, Duck," he yelled.

"Yeah, I know. Just get Billy."

"On three. One. Two. Heave!"

Jobs raised one of Billy's arms and shoved Billy Weir up and out of the water as hard as he could. Mo'Steel's hand caught Billy's stiff arm.

All at once Billy was up and Jobs was watching them bounce away.

Jobs sloshed toward where Wylson, Burroway, Violet, and Tate stood. It would be half an hour at least before Mo'Steel would be able to bring the Blimp back around.

They were an uncomfortable little group. Burroway hated the world, as far as Jobs could tell. He was a bitter man, weak and petulant. Miss Blake and her mother were not cozy at the best of times, and now Violet could barely conceal her loathing of a woman who admitted to having supported human sacrifice to the hideous baby.

As for Tate, Jobs had barely said a word to her. She was a nice-looking African-American girl with appraising eyes, a determined look, and a very cutting-edge hairstyle.

"Hi. I'm Jobs," he said and awkwardly held out his hand.

She shook it. "Tate. I'm from L.A."

"Monterey," Jobs said.

They shared wry grins at the weirdness of it. The references to hometowns that no longer existed, that hadn't existed for five centuries.

"I hear you get a lot of fog up there," Tate said.

Jobs nodded. "Yeah, but only down by the water. Besides, fog can be nice. The way it kind of —"

A metallic shriek of outrage killed the words.

"Riders," Jobs hissed. He stared hard toward the

island where the two Riders had let them walk away alive.

Tate nodded. "Yeah. That's a sound you don't need to hear twice."

"Maybe it's nothing," Wylson said, though she didn't look as if she believed her own words.

"There!" Burroway cried, pointing.

The two Riders were in view, now atop their hoverboards, floating at the edge of the island. All their attention was on the Blimp as it came around.

Again the sound of clashing steel gears and this time there came an almost instantaneous answering cry from an island a thousand yards off. An echo. Another. The cry was being taken up from all sides.

"It's because of the Blimps," Jobs said.

"Of course," Violet agreed. "Maybe some kind of sacrilege."

"Or maybe it's simpler than that," Tate said. "Maybe they're buffalo."

It took Jobs a second to process that idea. Of course. The Blimps, they could be prey animals. They could be the Riders' main source of food.

One thing was clear from the concentrated stares of the Riders: They didn't much approve of humans riding on the Blimps.

The two nearest Riders zoomed suddenly, leaning forward on their hoverboards.

Jobs felt their wind as they blew past, oblivious to everything but the approaching Blimp. He ducked instinctively.

The Riders flashed past and he could see them unlimbering their weapons.

"They're going to kill the Blimp!" Tate yelled.

Jobs knew it wasn't concern for the health of the Blimp. But if the Blimp was killed, the entire day's effort was wasted and the Riders might go on to slaughtering the humans.

"There goes Tamara!" Tate cried.

Tamara had run to the front of the Blimp. She still carried two Rider spears. The Riders were on the attack, ready to throw their javelins into the Blimp, and then they noticed Tamara. The Riders shifted aim and threw. In the same instant Tamara threw her spear, dodged one spear, caught another attacker's spear in midair, and laughed as one of the Riders was skewered through the neck of his eating head.

"Did you see that? Did you see her?" Tate cried giddily.

The speared Rider sheered away from the Blimp

but his board wobbled and he fell forward. He crashed into the Blimp and the spear in his neck stuck fast in the Blimp, pinning him like a butterfly in a display case.

The Blimp continued on toward Jobs and the others. But now Riders were vectoring in from other islands, racing to intercept.

"He's veering off! They're going to leave us!" Burroway yelled. "Get us! Get us out of here!" he cried.

"He's coming. Spread out!" Violet said. "We have to spread out."

"Everyone back from me," Wylson yelled. She shoved past Burroway to try and seize the first spot. Burroway grabbed her shoulder and spun her around.

Violet tried to get between her mother and the enraged scientist, but Burroway had already disengaged, accepting the second spot in line.

"Come on, I'll take the end spot," Jobs snapped.

Violet and Tate ran with him, ran directly away from the Blimp, hoping to spread out enough to allow each to be picked up. But the Riders were sure to foil the plan — they skimmed inches off the water, spears ready.

"Tamara will get them," Tate gasped as she ran.

"She's good, but she's not that good," Jobs grated. "Too many of them."

The Blimp was closing in on Wylson.

"Come on, Mom," Violet whispered. "Come on, you can do it."

(CHAPTER EIGHT)

"ACT AS IF IT'S REAL."

He had dreamed in the year 2011.

He had dreamed of a great and terrible emptiness spanning eternity.

And he had dreamed of a copper sea and of great, bouncing beasts as big as zeppelins.

During the time of silence, while he floated in the chasm between a dead past and an unimaginable future, he had crossed the line of madness many times. He had long since lost the capacity to judge what was real and what was not, what was seen by his eyes and what his mind alone saw. What was reality? He was the least able of any human being to know the answer.

But he remembered his dreams, even the ones he never really had. He remembered everything, and he remembered this one, this dream, from so long ago, from the past, from Earth, from a Billy Weir who was a child.

The dream of the copper sea, and the great, bounding beasts like pink elephants, and the wild-eyed boy in the rigging of a tall ship.

Yes, the circle was closing.

Billy had touched the mind of the Blue Meanie called Four Sacred Streams, had passed Jobs's words through himself and into the Meanie's mind. Or thought he had. Maybe that was imagined, not real.

He remembered drawing the life from his tortured father. Unless that, too, was merely a fragment of memory, a dream, a nightmare, his or some other person's.

But *this* he remembered. The copper sea. The bouncing beasts. He remembered from so long ago.

And now . . .

And now . . .

Billy felt himself picked up and hurled through the air. Rockets were strapped to his back and fired. He was a bullet blasted from the barrel of a gun.

The world tore past him, a blur, colors all run together, sounds all just shrieks and buzzing, felt as if his skin might be torn from his face by the sudden acceleration.

He wanted to scream. From dead stop to full

speed in a flash. He had floated, slowed, slowed almost to death, floated apart, above the world, distant from it, feeling it through gauze, hearing it through thick walls, seeing it through a reversed telescope.

Now he was a volcano eruption. An explosion. All distance shattered. The speed of the world matched by his own.

The circle was closed. Billy was back in sync.

He sat up.

He was atop the Blimp. No one noticed him; their backs were all turned away, all of them watching the Riders approaching.

He could feel their fear, so close and sharp and real. He could see their sudden, birdlike movements in real time. He could hear the words they spoke and understand them.

Billy Weir's hands rested on the spongy flesh of the Blimp. He touched the animal's mind as easily as he touched its skin.

A herd animal. Unafraid. It had no ingrained fear of humans. Nor even of the Riders.

It feared only one thing.

Billy tried to make sense of the half-aware, deeply stupid creature's memories. An image. A smell. A tingling in the air . . .

Lightning?

Billy formed the image of a bolt of lightning coming out of the sky, striking the Blimp, igniting the gas within. A fireball!

That's what the Blimp feared.

"Not yet," Billy whispered. "Not yet."

Then, to Tamara, or more exactly to the baby, he spoke in a clear voice. "Can you hold them off? If you can hold them off till we pick up the others, I can make this creature . . . hurry."

A dozen faces stared at him. Only Tamara's showed fear.

"Billy?" Mo'Steel said.

"I can make this creature go faster, Mo," Billy said. He felt unsure. Unsure even of whether he was actually speaking words, of whether indeed any of this was real.

"Act as if it's real," he whispered to himself.

"Act as if *what's* real?!" Mo'Steel demanded.

"Tamara. Do what you can," Billy urged.

The Marine sergeant looked confused. The baby bared its teeth at Billy and made a low, hissing sound. Then the baby's shrewd face closed in, its empty eye sockets looked away, and Tamara set the baby down on the living floor.

The baby spoke. Maybe. Maybe to Billy. Maybe

only to Billy, because Billy could see that no one else heard the baby's voice, no one else looked at it. Had it spoken? Billy had heard it.

He heard the baby say, "Stay out of my way."

"I am not your enemy," Billy whispered.

The baby snarled. "Be sure you don't become my enemy."

CHAPTER NINE

"THAT'S STILL A FART, DUCK."

Things happened all at once. Suddenly, and yet as if in slow motion, with each element clearly observed.

Tamara ran to the front and without pausing, launched a spear that flew faster than anything Mo'Steel had ever seen.

Wylson grabbed for the rope and slipped.

The spear hit the carapace of a Rider, failed to penetrate, but by sheer force of impact knocked him backward off his board.

A Rider threw a boomerang. The blade bounced off the hide of the Blimp and, with most of its speed lost, tumbled into Olga, who picked it up.

Wylson made a second, desperate grab, held on, and Anamull grabbed her arm and yanked her up brutally.

Tamara aimed and threw.

Burroway grabbed the rope.

The spear went in one of the large spider eyes of a Rider.

Burroway was being dragged through the water, yelling curses.

Mo'Steel flopped down, slid facedown, straight down the flabby wall of flesh, and caught himself with double handfuls of skin. He dug his knees in, snatched Burroway's shirt, it tore, Mo'Steel snatched again and grabbed an arm.

A pair of Riders were right there, right alongside, not three feet away, staring hate, drawing back to stab at Burroway.

Mo'Steel hauled with all his strength, felt 2Face holding onto his ankles, felt Burroway come up, saw the spear flash and strike a shallow stab into the Blimp.

Ahead, Tate, at the ready in the water, arms outstretched. Mo'Steel felt Burroway crawling up over him, gouging his kidneys with his heel.

A spear flew, two, three, all at once as a wave of Riders threw.

A cry of triumph from above, Tamara's voice, wild with glee.

A ripped-steel screech from the Riders.

Tate's hand. Grab. Not heavy, at least. Mo'Steel swung her up with the momentum, landed her to be grabbed by Yago.

He was worth something, at least, Yago was.

Now, for Violet.

But the Riders were concentrating their force dead ahead, just beyond where Jobs crouched. If the Riders charged they'd run right over Jobs. If the Blimp kept its direction it would surely bounce into the Riders.

Violet's hand, the missing finger, he gripped too tight, blood flowing anew from the stump, Violet gritting her teeth, slipping! Roger Dodger, just a kid, sliding down like Mo'Steel, facedown, using the friction to hold on, grabbed her other arm. Roger wasn't strong but he gave Mo'Steel the split second he needed to shift his grip and yank Violet up and away.

The Riders attacked! Full speed, shoulder to shoulder, seven of them in a tight formation looking for a head-on collision with the Blimp. They rode with spears held tight and raised, looking to slash the Blimp's underside on the next bounce.

"Duck!" Mo'Steel cried.

"What?!" Jobs yelled.

"No, *duck*! I mean, *duck*, Duck!"

Jobs dropped and buried his head in the water.

Mo'Steel grabbed the rope and swung out into the air, released, and splashed in the water, all but knocking Jobs down.

The Blimp jerked, suddenly rose.

Up, up, over their heads.

Inches from the upraised spear points of the Riders.

Mo'Steel dragged his friend's head up into the air, turned him around, and yelled, "Grab a leg!"

Like the propeller of a speedboat, the rows of cilia came rushing, churning the water, flailing madly.

The Riders raced on, sure they would gut the Blimp.

Jobs and Mo'Steel grabbed cilia. Mo'Steel was kicked in the face by his, wondered if he'd lost a tooth, felt the cilia go limp and passive, felt the wind billow beneath the Blimp, saw the water fall away below, saw the Riders gaping up, helpless, knew that he and Jobs were airborne, and knew it wasn't going to last.

The Blimps bounced, they didn't fly. This one had bounced right over the heads of the Riders, but it wasn't going to get away, not when the Riders could outrun it by twenty miles per hour to five.

"Who's flying this thing?" Jobs gasped.

"I think Billy is. Can you hold on?"

"We're coming back down!"

"Wrap your arms and legs around it," Mo'Steel yelled.

The water rushed up at them. The cilia/legs were already motoring, preparing to touch down. Glancing back, the Riders had turned and were in close pursuit. The rear of the Blimp dropped and hid them from view.

A shiver ran through the Blimp. More than a shiver, a convulsion, like the thing was going to throw up. The flabby skin gathered into wrinkles and folds. There was a sudden release, a very loud, recognizably embarrassing noise, and a burst of speed that shot the Blimp forward at twice its normal speed.

The descent stopped, the Blimp rose a dozen feet, and Mo'Steel saw the pursuing Riders wallowing in the water, their boards skimming away without them. They'd been knocked off.

"The Blimp farted?" Mo'Steel asked, incredulous.

"Must be some kind of pressure-release valve," Jobs said. "The gas pressure inside the Blimp must build up in the heat of the day."

"That's still a fart, Duck."

"How do we get up onto the Blimp?" Jobs asked.

They were dangling from the back third of a zeppelin, contemplating climbing up on top. Mo'Steel was always optimistic where the physically impossible was concerned, but it was still hard to see in what universe that was going to happen.

"Hey, we're going down!"

"Headfirst!"

The Blimp had suddenly plunged, not rear-down, but head-down at a sharp angle. Like a jet out of control and looking to dig a hole.

"Hang on!" Mo'Steel yelled. "It may work!"

"What? What may work?"

"Hang on!"

The Blimp hit the water "face" down. The shock of impact was absorbed by the gas balloon, squeezed the sides out, and tossed Mo'Steel and Jobs forward, clinging madly to their cilia.

Then the ball bounced.

The energy absorbed into the flesh of the Blimp now rebounded, bounced it up and over into a forward somersault of gargantuan proportions.

"Get ready!" Mo'Steel screamed. "Get ready to let go!"

"Say *what*?!"

The rear portion of the Blimp accelerated up as fast as a roller coaster coming off the first big drop. Mo'Steel and Jobs were yanked up at a shocking speed.

"Ready . . ."

The Blimp rolled ponderously forward into the somersault and came completely clear of the ground.

At the point of maximum centrifugal stress, Mo'Steel yelled, "Let go! Let go!"

Mo'Steel and Jobs released and flew high, spinning out of control through the air.

Beneath them the Blimp rotated, spun in midair, and fell. Mo'Steel and Jobs fell. Mo'Steel hit the trampoline flesh and grabbed frantic handfuls.

"Jobs! You okay?"

"I'm here," Jobs yelled, his voice shaky.

They were no longer on the bottom of the Blimp, they were on the side, almost all the way back, hanging on by their fingernails. The Blimp had completely reversed direction.

"Climb upward, Duck. Hand over hand. You can dig your knees in, especially now; the skin's looser after the big fart."

Mo'Steel glanced down and saw a solitary Rider keeping pace with the Blimp as it turned back onto its original heading once again. It was impossible to read any specific emotion on that utterly alien face, but Mo'Steel was prepared to guess that the Rider was astonished.

CHAPTER TEN

"WE HAVE TO TAKE IT AWAY FROM THEM. WE HAVE TO MAKE IT OURS."

"Billy? You okay?"

Billy Weir looked up at Jobs. His eyes were dark, but they moved. They focused. He was sitting very still, but he was at least sitting.

Jobs leaned closer. "Billy. You know me, right? You remember me?"

Billy frowned, looked unsure, like he was running through a mental list of possible answers, each more distressing than the last.

"I know you, Jobs," Billy said at last. His voice sounded strange. Halting. Vague.

"That was some impressive work back there," Mo'Steel said with a huge grin. "You're a serious Blimp pilot."

Billy stared blankly. He frowned and seemed to be thinking or remembering. Then his eyes darted to the left, avoiding contact.

"Well, anyway, thanks," Mo'Steel said. "You have any idea where we're going?"

"There's . . . there's a ship," Billy said. "Sails, anyway. I think so. I think maybe there's a ship. I dreamed it."

"Uh-huh," Jobs said dubiously. Billy might be awake and more or less alert, but he was still not exactly back to normal. In fact, he had the disconnected, off-center look of a street crazy. Back home, back in the world, Jobs would have crossed the street to steer clear of him.

"I'll decide where we go," Wylson Lefkowitz-Blake said, looming up behind Jobs. "It's something we need to discuss." She looked at Jobs. "We need a new spokesman for the youth. Yago will not be performing that duty any longer. I'm appointing you, Jobs."

"I don't speak for anyone but me," Jobs said.

"Burroway? Shy? Olga?" Wylson yelled. "You, too, T.R. We have to hold a board meeting. Tamara, of course you're welcome to attend as well."

Yago said, "You don't just decide to exclude me, Wylson."

"You're out," Wylson snapped.

"No, I don't think so."

"Jobs will represent the minors," Wylson said.

"No, I won't," Jobs said, growing testy at being referred to as if he weren't there.

"Put it to a vote," Yago purred. "You want to play games, Wylson, put it to a vote of the kids. Me and Jobs. Let's see who the people choose."

"You're calling a meeting?" Burroway demanded. "We're on the back of a Blimp in the middle of a swamp, Wylson."

"And going nowhere, Burroway. So let's meet, see if we can't formulate some options."

"You people are all nuts," Violet Blake said. "But if it's coming to a vote, I vote for Jobs."

"No one is voting," Jobs yelled.

"I vote for Yago," D-Caf said.

"Me, too," Anamull chimed in.

"You believe this?" Mo'Steel asked his friend.

"How about you, 2Face?" Yago asked.

She glanced at Jobs and hung her head. "I have to go with Yago."

"That's four votes for me, counting my own," Yago said. "Edward and Roger Dodger are too young to vote — besides, Edward is a mutant, and we don't let mutants vote."

Jobs looked up sharply. "What is your malfunction, Yago? Ten minutes ago we're all dead and now it's time to start playing divide and rule again? Can't you take a vacation?"

Yago returned Jobs's stare, unflinching. "We'll give you Miss Blake here, although what you see in him, Miss Blake, is beyond me. Plus you've got your monkey-boy pal and your own vote. That's three. Leaves just Tate, and all she can do is give you a tie, Jobs."

"Billy has a vote," Jobs pointed out.

"Mutant," Yago said with a self-satisfied grin. "A freak of nature."

Jobs met his gaze and felt himself flinch, though he didn't show it. Jobs knew what he was: a techie. Techies were respected in his old school, but they weren't on a par with guys like Yago. Yago was bigger, stronger, richer, famous, cocky, and inhumanly good-looking. He was the President's son. Never mind that the President had been dead for five hundred years, that she'd been President of a nation that no longer existed and a prominent member of a species that just barely existed. Yago was still Yago, and Jobs was still just Jobs.

Jobs was sure he'd hidden his internal surrender, but Wylson at least must have seen it.

"How about this: You're *both* in," Wylson said. "Jobs, you're in. Yago, I can't seem to get rid of you, so you're in, too. Now let's get on with this meeting. I want a clear agenda."

2Face started laughing to herself, a low chuckle, but one that gained momentum. "This is insane. This is just insane. We're all crazy."

T.R. said, "I think you should leave mental health diagnoses to the experts. That would be me."

"Oh, shut up, you fatuous nitwit," 2Face said through the laughter. "Ms. Lefkowitz-Blake, no offense, I'm sure you were a great business tycoon or whatever, but right now you're not being very smart. Hold a meeting? Look around you. We're a handful of scruffy, raggedy, smelly, dirty humans sitting on the back of a giant bouncing hippopotamus, wandering around lost inside an alien spaceship so big it could hold a million people. And you're going to formulate a plan? Like what we really need is a business plan to present at the next shareholders' meeting?" She jerked a thumb at Yago. "And this fool thinks what we really need is to split up into factions? And we've got some psychotic Marine sergeant with an alien baby and, no offense, some creepy kid who just woke up out of a coma who's doing a mind-meld with this gasbag we're on, and Riders and Blue Meanies and living artworks and . . . and you want an *agenda?*"

As she talked the laughter stopped and now the untouched half of her melted face was red with anger and contempt.

"We're not big enough or strong enough or smart enough to have an agenda. We're trapped inside the universe's biggest video game and we don't even get to touch the game pad. Since we woke up from hibernation, how many have died? Set aside the Missing Eight. How many have died?"

No one answered her.

She held up her fingers. "The doctor, Connie Huerta. Killed by the baby. Errol, massacred by Riders. Billy's dad, eaten by worms. Three dead since we woke up. And everyone injured to one degree or another. The rest of us alive. By luck."

"You have a point?" Burroway demanded.

"Yeah, I have a point," 2Face said. "We're not a company, Ms. Lefkowitz-Blake. And we're not the White House, Yago. And we're not high school, Miss Blake. And we're not at some university, Burroway, and we're not a family, Dad, and we're not on some kind of thrill ride, Mo."

Jobs shook himself out of a spell cast by her

words and face. He glanced around and saw that everyone, absolutely everyone, the entire human race, he thought mordantly, was listening. No one was listening more intently than the baby.

"We came here on the Mayflower Project. Maybe that ought to tell us something," 2Face said, quiet now. "We're the human race. All of it, as far as we know. Strangers in the strangest land anyone ever saw. But as strange as it is, it's all we have." She waved her arms around, encompassing the vista of swamps, the Blimp herd, the Riders watching from afar. "They own this place now. Mother does. The Riders. The Meanies, maybe. Maybe others we don't know about yet. We have to take it away from them. We have to make it ours. Kill them all if we have to: Mother, the Riders, the Meanies. Anyone else who tries to stop us." She paused, obviously spent. With a sigh, she added, "You want an agenda? *That's* our agenda."

2Face took a deep breath, collecting herself, and walked away. She passed close by Yago, and only he and Jobs could see the look of triumph in her eye.

No meeting took place. The Blimp bounded on, hour after hour, pursued, kept in view by a tag team of Riders. Billy kept the Blimp moving, long after the rest of the huge, comical herd had slowed and stopped to rest.

Jobs was thinking, his mind far away when he felt 2Face touch his arm.

"You know why I had to vote with Yago," she said.

"No. I don't," Jobs said. "But it doesn't matter."

"Yago is the enemy here. As much as the Riders or anything else," 2Face said. "He's very clever. He wants an 'us against them' thing, normal people, as he defines them, versus freaks. He needs there to be factions."

"Yeah, I get that," Jobs said.

"He never expected to win a vote. It wasn't about voting. It was about him finding an excuse to say 'Freak,' or 'Mutant.' That's his game. Any chance he gets. So I voted for him, left him the choice of either rejecting me as a freak or accepting me as a supporter. He was too slow: He accepted my vote, gave me credibility in his little scheme."

She smiled with the good half of her mouth. Jobs wondered what it would be like to kiss her and instantly felt a wave of revulsion. Not for her face, but for her. She had saved Edward, looked out for him. But 2Face was as shifty as Yago.

In part to cover for the unexpected feelings of antipathy, Jobs said, "That was some speech you gave before. Kill them all?"

2Face nodded. Again the slight, sly smile. "Was I wrong?"

"Four Sacred Streams saved us all by giving his own life," Jobs answered.

"He gave his life for his own cause," 2Face said.

"You said it yourself, Mother is a big place. Maybe we can all fit. Us, the Riders, the Meanies."

2Face shook her head. "No. Only we can fit. And not even all of us, Jobs." She looked pointedly at Yago, lying down for a rest, and then at Tamara, who stood, with baby on hip, gazing out over the landscape.

"So you play the same game as Yago."

"No. I'm one of the good guys, Jobs, just like you. I just don't like losing."

CHAPTER ELEVEN

"GOOD NIGHT, BEULAH."

It was strange to be happy, Mo'Steel realized. But there was no point in denying feelings. He was happy.

Jobs wasn't, that was the only crab. If Jobs was down, it was hard for Mo'Steel to feel too up.

Of course there were other problems: the infighting between Yago and 2Face; the tension between Miss Blake and her mother; and of course, the great crushing weight of tragedy that hung over them all.

Then there were the Riders.

But, man, riding the Big Balloon, bouncing across the exotic swampy wasteland, an alien wind in his face, the memory of thrills that had nearly ruptured his A gland . . . It was good.

The landscape had begun to change. The watery vistas had given way to a sea of yellow grass cut through by endless, wandering streams and dotted with clumps of shaky trees.

He perched as far forward on the Blimp as he could, spread his arms wide to feel the breeze, feel the speed, feel the weird slow bouncing, feel the unusual, the bizarre, the amazing, the never-seen-before, life-hanging-on-by-its-fingernails thrill.

"You think we'll stop when it gets dark?"

Mo'Steel opened his eyes and saw that the question had come from Tate.

"I don't know," Mo'Steel said. "Maybe the sky pilot back there knows." He indicated Billy Weir. "Or maybe Beulah will tell us."

"Beulah?"

"The Blimp." He grinned. "The Big Balloon. Beulah the Bouncing Bag."

Tate smiled back at him, a nice smile. "You get off on this, don't you?"

"You have to take it minute by minute," Mo'Steel answered. "People mess up extending too far forward or back. You go far enough back, far enough forward, you're always going to find something to feel bad about. But if you keep it all on local time, stay present tense, hey, ninety percent of right now is good."

"The threads of past and future run through the present," Tate said.

"Who said that?" Mo'Steel wondered.

"Me. I said it."

"It sounded good. Like maybe it was a famous quote. Anyway, though, it's not right. The future doesn't exist, not yet. Neither does the past, not anymore. All you know for sure is right now, *compañero*. And right now, this is good, isn't it?"

Tate looked skeptical. "This plus a hot shower, food, a big glass of fresh-squeezed orange juice, that would be good."

"No, that would be perfect," Mo'Steel admitted with a laugh.

For a while they were silent, standing close but not very close. They rode the bounce, knees taking the rippling shock, absorbing the upswell, enjoying the slight sensation of weightlessness at the top of each low arc.

"Mo? I can call you Mo, right?"

"Sure."

"What do you think about her? Them."

Mo'Steel had to turn his head to see who Tate was talking about. She was looking at Tamara and the baby, who were riding comfortably toward the rear, behind the main knot of people.

"I don't know," Mo'Steel admitted and felt a bit of his inner glow dim. "The baby creeps me out."

Tate said nothing and seemed not to have heard. "You know what I think? I mean, no, what I *feel?*"

Mo'Steel said nothing. Tate wanted to talk, he'd let her. Although he regretted the loss of his carefree moment.

"I feel there's a connection between Tamara and the baby that's not like anything anyone knows about. And I have the same feeling that there's a connection between the baby and Billy Weir. I can't . . . I can't touch it. It's like when you join a group of people who were already talking among themselves, and they're polite to you, they talk to you and all, but it's like you can feel an echo of a conversation that was going on before you showed up and is going to continue after you leave."

"Billy worries the sergeant," Mo'Steel agreed.

"Tamara and the baby on one end, Billy Weir on the other. But I don't feel like that's all of it. I don't feel like it's a line, two sides. It's not a seesaw. I feel like it's a triangle. I feel like there's a third person balancing things."

"Yeah?"

Tate aimed her dark eyes at Mo'Steel and he felt a squirming discomfort.

"Yeah, Mo. You."

He shook his head. "I'm just me, Tate. I'm not anything more or different or whatever. I'm just me."

Tate winked. "Yeah, I know. Everyone else has an agenda, even your friend Jobs. And everyone else has an ax to grind, another dimension to them. Only not you. You're exactly what you are, aren't you?"

Mo'Steel laughed. "I guess I am."

Tate shrugged. "Hey, at least it's not cold, huh? Nice and warm. Like any L.A. evening."

She left Mo'Steel to ponder her words, but he didn't. Instead he wondered if he should go to sleep. The sun was plunging toward a horizon that was maybe not exactly real. He was tired. His mom was already curling up and resting her head on her arms. Billy was driving. Jobs was in one of his occasional contemplative funks, writing poetry in his head.

"Might as well sleep," Mo'Steel decided. "Good night, Beulah."

CHAPTER TWELVE

"IT'S GOING TO END HERE."

The sun rose. A new day.

Violet Blake had slept surprisingly well. She was ravenous and thirsty. But the flabby, living balloon made a soft bed, and she had needed sleep even more than food or drink.

She woke and took stock of her fairly pitiful condition: Her dress was a wreck, literally falling apart, shredded and decayed. It was on the edge of being immodest.

There was dirt under her fingernails. And more troubling, she had only nine fingernails. The wound where her missing finger had been seemed finally to have stopped seeping blood. There was a hideous crust of scab, but when she looked at it she didn't see the pus or bright redness that would indicate infection. Nor did she feel feverish.

Her hair . . . Forget the hair, it was a dirty mop stuck on her head.

Shampoo, such a simple thing. Back home she'd had about three different brands. Aveda. That's what she wanted. A bottle of Aveda shampoo. Plus a new finger or at least a decent bandage.

Her mother was already awake, of course, and striding back and forth putting on a show of being in charge and concerned. Yago was sitting up, scratching his leaf-green hair till he realized he was being watched. He gave Violet an insolent leer and she looked away, simultaneously revolted and flattered.

Maybe her hair didn't look so bad.

Billy Weir sat still, eyes open, but with a stricken look of exhaustion. He was sweating despite a morning chill in the air. He looked as if he might at any moment lapse back into his coma.

Violet stood up, wobbled slightly as she missed the rhythm of the bounce, mistaking a bottoming for a rebound.

The Blimp felt strange. It shuddered. There was a gentle lurch, almost as if the beast had missed a step, almost tripped.

Then she stared, and blinked, and stared again.

The landscape had changed, all grass now, endless fields of grass, like unnaturally yellow wheat or sea grass. The streams no longer appeared.

But that wasn't what stopped her heart from beating. Two hundred Riders, maybe more, maybe less, but far more Riders than they had ever seen before, were following in their wake. They rode their boards at grass-top level, surfing the wheat.

So many. Far too many.

Tamara held the baby on her hip and glared back at them. There was tension in her every fiber. Her face was an angry mask, but anger covering fear. The languid cockiness Tamara had always shown when facing the Riders was gone.

"We're in for it now," D-Caf remarked, then giggled nervously.

Yago spotted their pursuers and, Violet thought, nearly fainted.

Jobs had his hand on Edward's shoulder, comforting, reassuring. Edward was barely distinguishable, having long since adopted the coloration of the Blimp.

"There are too many," Tate said. "She can't do it. Not even she can fight this and win."

The rim of the sun popped over the horizon quite suddenly, and the dim dawn light blazed brighter.

The Riders screamed a fierce welcome. The noise was a wave that rippled through the exhausted skin of the Blimp.

"I don't think we're going to Blimp-fart our way out of this," Olga Gonzalez said in a flat attempt at humor.

"Here they come," Burroway said without affect.

The Riders surged forward, picked up speed, leaned forward on their boards. It was a sea of mouth/heads, like ravenous worms, the main, insect-eyed heads intent, focused on their target.

It's going to end here, Violet thought with deep sadness. *The human race died on this unknown date, in this unknown place, at the hands of these monstrous creatures.*

"She's weakening." Billy's voice was a harsh croak. "She's dying. Needs to rest."

Violet knelt beside him. "Who? Beulah? I mean, the Blimp?"

"I've pushed her too long. We won't make it. Another few minutes at most."

"I'll tell . . ." Who? Who should she tell? Her mother? Jobs? "Billy, is there anything we can do?"

"Maybe. Go inside. Hide inside her."

"What?"

"Make as small a hole as possible. The healing will draw strength away, but it may help."

"You're telling me we can crawl inside this Blimp?"

Billy nodded, then his head slumped forward onto his chest and he might have been dead but for the fact that sweat still seeped from his forehead.

Violet jumped up. "Jobs! Where are you?"

A Rider boomerang sliced through the air, veered just inches from her face, and flit-flitted around on its return trip.

"They'll be in range soon," Jobs said grimly, appearing at her side.

"Jobs. Listen to me. Billy says we can cut our way inside. Inside the Blimp. But the Blimp is dying."

Another boomerang fluttered by. They were clearly still at the extreme range of the Riders' primitive weapons. But that situation wouldn't last.

Jobs yelled, "Sergeant!"

Tamara snapped her head around with a poisonous look that mirrored the baby's expression.

"Billy says we can get inside the Blimp," Violet told her.

Tamara nodded curtly, as if this was not news to her, but merely an unwelcome reminder. The Marine sergeant searched the forward horizon, seemed to be taking her bearings, then knelt to touch the skin of the Blimp. She glared at the pursuing Riders.

The baby stared daggers at Billy. The eyeless sockets aimed directly at him and the tiny mouth bared teeth in a snarl.

"Okay," Tamara said. "Get everyone here."

Tamara made the cut. It was a two-foot-long slit. The lips of the cut flapped as the gas began escaping.

"Keep the opening spread or it'll reseal itself," Tamara ordered. Then, without waiting, she slid down, feetfirst, through the hole, holding the baby up above her head. Once the baby was inside, Violet and Jobs each grabbed a side of the cut.

"Everyone go!" Jobs yelled. "Go, go, go!"

Anamull was next.

Then the Riders saw what was happening and set up a murderous shrieking. They no longer kept to a line — the faster Riders surged forward, eating up the distance.

A dozen boomerangs flew.

"Drop!" 2Face shouted.

Most fell on their faces. Only Burroway and Edward failed to respond. Only by dumb luck did the boomerangs miss them. Jobs grabbed his brother and yanked him down. Burroway stood paralyzed, white-faced, realizing only belatedly how close he'd come to being sliced up.

"Down, you jackass!" Olga shouted and rolled

into him, collapsing his knees just as a new covey of boomerangs converged where he had stood.

Panic set in. Everyone wanted into the slit. Yago elbowed past Roger Dodger, pushing the smaller boy aside. They crawled over and around each other, grabbing at the slit.

"One at a time," Violet yelled.

The Riders were closing in all around. And suddenly, there was one of them, face just peeking into view as he climbed the side of the Blimp.

Mo'Steel gave a wild yell and trampolined into the Rider. The Rider fell backward and almost carried Mo'Steel with him.

Wylson squirmed up next to Violet. "Get in, Dallas," she said. "I'll hold the flap."

Violet flinched at the use of her given name. "No, Mom, you go."

Wylson rose up, wrapped her arms around her daughter from behind, and shoved hard. They fell together through the hole and into the Blimp.

(CHAPTER THIRTEEN)

"DO THESE BOARDS ROCK, OR WHAT?"

Three Riders appeared, climbing up the side of the Blimp. Jobs saw them. Mo'Steel was out of sight, maybe already fallen, maybe dead, Jobs didn't know. Things were happening too fast.

Jobs felt a moment of cold fear. He hesitated. Attack, he knew he had to attack, but he froze, unable to move, told himself he was a coward, told himself he was needed to hold open the flap for Billy and Mo'Steel, cursed himself for being weak, and then, in a rush that occurred before his brain had formed the decision, he was up and running full tilt at the Riders.

He ran on rubber legs, brain disconnected from his body, wrapped his arms around his head, and plowed blindly into where the Rider had been.

The Rider easily sidestepped him and Jobs barreled, unstoppable, off the side of the Blimp.

He shouted and hit facedown on something hard yet giving.

He saw a flash of sky, of the wildly agitated grass, of the wall-sided Blimp, all of it tumbling together.

He rolled and almost fell off the hoverboard.

"Hoverboard?" he asked.

Jobs grabbed at air, twisted over, and hugged the edges of the hoverboard as if his life depended on it.

Riders were suddenly zooming all around him, stabbing with their short spears.

"Go!" Jobs screamed and the board shot forward. Not fast enough — the Riders were everywhere. He slid to the right and the board veered wildly. It plowed into the close-packed ranks of Riders. It was dominoes tumbling. The Riders ran into one another and at least three ended up hitting the grass, unboarded.

The board stabilized but not in a good way. Jobs caught a glimpse of a Rider hanging on the side of the Blimp. The Rider had one hand extended toward Jobs, and the board was veering swiftly back toward him.

Mind control, Jobs realized. The hoverboards were mind-controlled. As long as the board's owner lived, no one else could control his board.

The hoverboard carried Jobs swiftly to the waiting spear of its owner.

Then Mo'Steel appeared, running, bounding, and stabbed a spear through the Rider, back to front.

Jobs had the weird thought that now he knew what a Rider looked like when he was surprised. The skewered Rider fell away, and hit the grass.

Mo'Steel took a bounce on the Blimp's side, somersaulted through the air, and slammed with bone-crunching force into a Rider keeping pace with the Blimp.

The Rider tumbled off his board, fell backward, and Mo'Steel held on by his fingernails. He hauled himself aboard the hoverboard, knelt to get his balance, then jumped upright.

"Good idea, Duck!" Mo'Steel yelled. "Take their boards! Yaaaaaah!"

Jobs, who was still clinging to his own board, could only groan.

The Riders had all but forgotten the Blimp now, focused as they were on eliminating the two hoverboard thieves.

Mo'Steel's mount was fighting him, moving to return to its owner. Jobs's board now belonged to him. He tried to stand but he was trembling too much and could only crouch on his knees. Still, he found he could shift his weight and turn the machine left or right, and that he could think, *Faster* or *Slower*, and get the desired result.

He tried to intercept Mo'Steel's board, which was now zooming at top speed back to its injured but living owner.

Jobs could see the injured Rider standing tall, spear held forward. He was calling his board to him and would impale Mo'Steel.

Jobs aimed for the Rider and called for all the speed the board could handle. A surge of Riders raced to cut him off. No, he'd make it, no, he wouldn't, yes, no — the injured Rider had spotted him!

Jobs scooted, inches away from pursuers, and slammed the injured Rider at neck level. The jolt sent Jobs flying. He tumbled, arms and legs everywhere, and hit the ground shoulder first. The hoverboard kept flying.

The grass softened the landing but he was winded and decided to pretty much just crouch there and hope no one saw him.

"Jump!" a voice bellowed and Jobs, for once in his life, reacted instantly.

He jumped straight up, like he was going for a jump shot. Mo'Steel's arm caught him around the chest, crushed the last of the air from his lungs, and yanked him up and away.

"Do these boards rock, or what?" Mo'Steel yelled, his mouth right at Jobs's ear.

They zoomed away, running parallel again with the Blimp and millimeters ahead of the whole angry swarm of Riders.

Jobs didn't feel exultant. The Riders would inevitably catch them. The Blimp was failing, sagging, slowing.

And there was no way they would make it to the open, blue sea. . . .

The what? Jobs wondered stupidly.

CHAPTER FOURTEEN

"I THINK WHATEVER'S IN HERE IS GETTING TO US."

2Face slid facedown into the slit. She felt the breeze of the boomerangs on her legs and then she was in.

The inside of the Blimp was not quite what she expected. It was not a single, vast gasbag. It was more like a human lung. She and most of the others huddled within a roughly spherical chamber perhaps twenty feet in diameter. The chamber was open at the bottom and to one side, open through what could only be described as sphincters.

In fact, 2Face realized with the beginning of a giggle, they were definitely sphincters. They'd open and close, allowing more gas in or out, each time squeezing shut like a . . . well, like a sphincter.

"Sphincter," 2Face said in a weird, mouse voice. She laughed.

Yago erupted in high-pitched Munchkin laughter. "Total sphincter."

"I thought you were the biggest sphincter I'd ever seen, Yago, but these are bigger," 2Face said. Then, listening to the weird quality of her own voice she added, " 'Follow the yellow brick road.' "

Yago laughed. Everyone laughed. In fact, every face was split by a big, idiot grin. The only exceptions were Tamara and the baby.

" 'We represent the Lollipop Guild,' " Burroway sang, off-key.

Wylson held up her hand, trying to get control of the group. "I think we should . . . We should . . ." She frowned and then grinned and then shrugged. "I don't know what we should do."

"Hey. You know what?" 2Face said.

"What?" Violet asked, just as serious.

"Um . . . I don't remember."

Violet grinned. "Me, neither."

"Helium. And nitrous oxide," Olga said. "Other gases, too."

"Huh?"

"I think the gas in this . . . Um . . ." Olga began, and then evidently lost her train of thought.

"You know who was great?" Yago asked no one in particular. "That guy . . . the funny one. You know?"

Anamull nodded solemnly. "Curly."

"Yeah!" Yago said, snapping his fingers. "Only his name was Dave."

"Curly's name was Dave?"

"I think whatever's in here is getting to us," 2Face said.

"Nitrous oxide," Olga agreed. "Laughing gas."

"The Blimp is failing," Tamara said. "We should be ready to get out."

She wasn't laughing, but she did sound as much like a Munchkin as anyone.

2Face was working on something funny to say when a spear pierced the flesh wall behind her and stopped, quivering sluggishly.

"Whoa," she said.

"Follow me," Tamara grated.

"*She* is fine," Tate confided to 2Face with a finger to her lips.

Tamara slid through the horizontal opening into the next chamber, carrying the baby easily in the crook of one muscular arm.

"Let's go."

"'We represent the Lollipop Guild and we we-e-elcome you to Munchkin Land.'"

The Blimp was dying, Billy knew that. He could feel it as if it were happening to him. He had driven the

Blimp far past the limits of its strength. If he drove it any further he would kill it.

"I'm sorry," he whispered.

The question was whether he, himself, would survive the Blimp's death. Did the connection go both ways? Did the Blimp reach into him as he had reached into it? Could the Blimp die and yet leave Billy alive?

He wasn't very much afraid of death. There had been too many times when he'd begged for death, prayed to an absent God for the gift of death.

And even if he survived the Blimp's end, there was the baby. The baby hated him. Feared him. Billy didn't know why, but he felt it, a seething, relentless malice.

But that was okay, too. Maybe the baby would kill him. Maybe not. Maybe death, maybe life. Maybe the line wasn't as sharp and clear as that.

Still, he'd like to see the ships.

He opened his eyes. The Blimp's vision, which he had shared, was strange and wonderful in its own way, but not very useful. Better to look through his own eyes now. Not that he could be sure of what he saw even then.

Was that the sea? Was that not blue? A very Earthly blue?

He felt, through the Blimp's skin, the wild, running battle between Mo'Steel and Jobs and the Riders. He was aware, the way a human might feel his tummy rumbling, that people were moving around within the Blimp.

If the Blimp died, the gas would be released in a rush. The collapsing air sacs would trap those inside.

Had to keep it alive. Had to keep it moving toward that hallucination of an ocean, toward that blue mirage.

"I'm sorry," Billy said again.

The Blimp had no words to answer, barely a thought at all. It was tired. Puzzled. Why couldn't it stop? Why couldn't it rest? The Blimp was only vaguely self-aware. It never knew when it crossed the line between possible recovery and certain death.

Billy drove the Blimp forward, feeding his own power into it, draining himself with the effort.

The Blimp's cilia kicked and it bounded forward again.

CHAPTER FIFTEEN

"I SURFED HURRICANE TONYA BACK IN '09."

One minute they were skimming across copper streams and waving grass. The next minute they saw ahead of them deep, blue-green sea, foam-tipped waves, and strange statues rising up amid the waves.

Jobs and Mo'Steel reached the boundary between environments and their board fell like a stone. They plunged into icy water. Jobs tasted salt.

He bobbed to the surface just in time to see the Blimp collapse with a final shudder. It wallowed like a Macy's Parade balloon that had been half-deflated.

Billy Weir toppled from high atop the Blimp and rolled down the side into the water. Mo'Steel swam toward him, fighting three-foot waves.

Jobs treaded water. The cold would render him numb eventually, he knew. This was not the warm, shallow sea of the Rider default environment. They had entered a new nodal zone, a new environment. And this felt like ocean — deep and cold and rough.

The Riders had all stopped at the edge of their environment. He could see them hovering, watching, frustrated, but either unable or unwilling to cross the boundary. After a while they began to turn away.

Where were all the others? Jobs saw Mo'Steel holding onto Billy, keeping his head above water, but where were the others?

A horrible thought: Had they fallen off? Were they back in Rider territory?

Then a gash appeared in the back end of the droopy, sodden Blimp. Tamara appeared first, with the baby. The others piled out after her, laughing.

Mo'Steel was back with an unconscious Billy in tow.

"Are they laughing?" Mo'Steel demanded, incredulous and a bit offended.

"Seems like," Jobs said.

They plunged into the sea, one after another. But when they came up for air they weren't laughing anymore.

Billy Weir opened his red-rimmed eyes. He looked horribly weary, haggard. Mo'Steel continued to support him as the three of them made their way to the others.

"What . . ." Wylson began, then choked when she caught a mouthful of salt water.

"New environment," Jobs said. "Mother has all these nodes, right? Back there in Rider country that was the default because we'd destroyed that node. Destroy the node and the region controlled by the node goes to its default. But now we're in a new nodal zone, new environment."

"The Riders dropped back," Violet pointed out.

"I think maybe it's a territorial thing," Jobs suggested.

"We're going to freeze pretty soon," Yago said through chattering teeth.

"I saw statues or something when we were coming out of the Blimp," 2Face said, shivering.

"Me, too, just ahead. Can we make it?" Burroway worried.

"Let's get going," Wylson decided. Then she hesitated, looked at the Blimp, folds of its flesh rippling in the breeze. "Is there any way we can use this thing?"

"I think we used it all it could stand," Tate said.

Tamara, with the baby on her back, was already

swimming powerfully. The rest fell in behind her, breasting the waves as well as they could. It was very quickly obvious who the strong swimmers were and who could do little more than tread water. Billy was swimming on his own, somewhat recovered, so Jobs and Mo'Steel and Tate helped the frightened Anamull and sluggish Olga.

Once clear of the Blimp, the nearest of the statues came into view. It was an amazing sight, utterly out of place. A statue of a man, all white marble. Jobs guessed that it towered close to a hundred feet above the waves. It rested on a pedestal. When the waves hit, they crashed up and over the top of the pedestal and foamed around the statue's ankles.

"Looks familiar," Jobs gasped between mouthfuls of water.

"It's *David*," Violet said, managing to sound amazed at his ignorance even while gargling.

"Some painting?"

"A *painting*? You don't know David? Michelangelo's *David*?"

"I've heard of Michelangelo," Jobs said defensively.

"It's David," Violet sputtered. "You know, as in Goliath?"

"What's it doing in the middle of the ocean?"

"Mother's mixing media," Violet said. "Painting. Sculpture. Together."

They swam on and Jobs contemplated this fact as well as he could while dragging a nearly useless, shivering, chattering, fear-babbling Anamull along with him. Mother was mixing media? Combining images derived from the data stores on the shuttle?

That couldn't be good news. At least an environment derived from a painting might have some internal consistency. What if she started mixing elements of painting with photography? Good lord, he didn't want to think about some of the photos that Mother may have downloaded into her database. Human history was full of horrors captured on film.

The waves that were manageable out in the open were much less so up close to the statue's base. A three-foot wave made an amazing impact when it was suddenly stopped by a marble wall.

It was obvious to Jobs that it was going to be terribly difficult to get everyone up to the relative safety of the platform. Maybe impossible.

Jobs felt his strength beginning to ebb. The cold was like a drug. Like when he'd gone under general anesthetic to have his pancreas replaced.

He felt fear like a knife in his stomach. They were

going to die here, wallowing in the icy water. Even if they managed to climb atop the platform, so what? There was no food up there, no shelter. Plenty of water, but it was all salty, deadly to drink.

Jobs released Anamull without realizing he'd done it and sank beneath the surface. It was quiet down there. Down under the surface. All those legs kicking, all those billowing garments.

He watched, as if from far away, as his own mind argued over the relative merits of just continuing to sink or trying to survive only to die later. There was something to be said for having control over the fatal moment.

Everyone looked strange, disconnected from him. Just a bunch of kicking legs. They were all going to die, anyway. They didn't deserve to survive. The human race should have died out entirely five hundred years earlier. This was just a mockery of *H. sapiens*.

Then his air ran out and in a panic he surged back upward. The fear adrenaline gave his muscles a temporary new lease on life.

They were close to David's pedestal, close enough to feel the way the sea surged upward as it pressed against the base. He grabbed Anamull's shoulder. "Sorry, man."

"We have to ride the wave in," Mo'Steel gasped from not too far away.

"We'll be squashed like bugs," Burroway moaned.

"I can't do it," Shy Hwang cried pitifully. "I can't even feel my legs."

2Face swam to her father, a gesture, Jobs assumed, of filial love. He was wrong.

"Dad, shut up," 2Face snapped. "You, too, Burroway. All we get is whining from you. From both of you!"

Her father gaped, his round head like a cork on the water. Burroway looked like he was trying to gather up his dignity and deliver a stinging retort, but 2Face cut him off.

"Anyone wants to die, fine, die. Not me," she said. "I'm riding the next good wave in. If I can do it, so can the rest of you."

"You know how to do this?" Mo'Steel asked her dubiously.

"Swim team, Mo," 2Face said tersely. "And I surf."

"Where, on those lame little ripples you get down in Florida?" Mo'Steel teased. "Those aren't waves."

"I surfed Hurricane Tonya back in '09," 2Face said.

Mo'Steel laughed. "All right, *hermana,* let's do it together."

The combination of 2Face's grim determination and Mo'Steel's devil-may-care excitement exerted a calming influence on the soggy and shivering refugees. Jobs, like all the others, found himself fascinated, able to shut out for the moment the question of his own survival. If Mo'Steel and 2Face made it, maybe they all would make it.

2Face and Mo'Steel waited, glancing over their shoulders, judging the swell, waiting, waiting, then a nod of mutual agreement.

They took off, swimming hard, arm over arm, legs churning, matching speed with the onrushing wave. 2Face was almost too fast, she threatened to get ahead of the crest and slide down the slope. She pulled back, matched speed with Mo'Steel, rose on the swollen wave, and shot forward. There came the crash and thunder of thousands of gallons of water breaking green and white across the platform.

It was impossible to see anything at first. Then the wave receded and there they were, clinging to David's marble feet. There was a bright smear of red on 2Face's lip, washed away by the salt water draining from her hair.

Mo'Steel stayed on the platform, but 2Face

jumped back in to help guide the others in, one at a time.

It was a race against time. The cold was taking its toll. People stopped talking, conserving energy. Faces turned a pale blue. Hands were dead, feet might as well be amputated.

By the time he was hauled aboard the platform, Jobs felt more dead than alive. He had helped others to escape, always claiming to be fine, claiming he was good. And he was at first, living on the fear of his near-surrender. But then he started losing it, losing touch not only with his body but with his mind. At some point he was no longer in this artificially created ocean, but back in Monterey, back under the buttery sunlight, warm, out in the backyard, lawn chair, soda, tunes playing . . .

Mo'Steel's grip was like iron, fingers digging painfully into Jobs's upper arms. "Come on, 'migo, come on, be okay now."

Jobs returned to a consciousness only slightly warmer. He was buried within a heap of bodies, arms and legs everywhere. He was cuddled between Olga and Violet. Body heat. That was it. They were all trying to regain some warmth.

The sun helped. The sky was mostly clear except for some scattered puffs of white cloud. The sunlight helped, and the bodies packed around him helped, but then would come a wave washing over them and everyone would shiver again.

Jobs still couldn't feel his hands, but he wanted to stand up, to see what was what. He tried to move, but realized that he was providing warmth and protection to the others as much as they were to him.

No one talked. Someone was moaning. Violet's pale face was close to his own; he was breathing her breath. Her eyes were closed. When the wave came she flinched.

Jobs twisted his stiff neck and looked up. The statue was overwhelming. The legs were like tree trunks. Despite himself, Jobs laughed. It was idiotic, an absurd place to die.

"Sail!" a voice cried. "I see a sail. More than one."

CHAPTER SIXTEEN

"IT'S A BEAUTIFUL MACHINE, BUT IT'S JUST A MACHINE."

The ship came on, gliding, breasting the waves, its mountain of sails full. Was it heading for them, or just passing by? Was it a rescue, or just happenstance?

Violet Blake hoped for rescue. Mother owed them, didn't she? Or it?

The sea had calmed at last. The waves no longer crashed over the platform. No one was exactly dry yet and no one was likely to be dry as long as the stinging salt spray was carried on the wind. But no one was in danger of freezing any longer. The sun was out. The marble was cold but not icebox cold. If only the wind would die out, they might even achieve some degree of warmth. But then again, if the wind died, the ship would stop.

All eyes were on the ship. Mo'Steel had managed

to climb to David's knee, and he kept watch from beneath his shading hand.

"I still don't see anyone on it," he reported.

"You know anything about this?" Jobs asked Violet, coming up behind her.

"Not really. There were an awful lot of paintings done with sailing ships and vast expanses of open ocean. Could be any of them. Mother could have downloaded a thousand paintings from our data."

"I know that statue over there," Jobs said.

"*The Thinker?*" Violet asked wearily. "I think everyone knows that statue, Jobs."

The famous Rodin statue was about a mile off, maybe a little less. It was simply planted in the ocean. A muscular male figure bent forward, elbow on knee, chin on fist, thinking.

"See that one?" Violet pointed. "That's called *The Fourteen-Year-Old Dancer.* It's by Degas. The original's a bit smaller."

"It's all pretty creepy," Jobs said.

"I just hope the ship doesn't run into the *Dancer.*"

"I don't like Mother doing this," Jobs muttered.

Violet didn't ask him what he meant. She liked Jobs, but the guy was only really talkative when the subject was computers and if she got him started . . . She had no interest in computers, not even in Mother — assuming Mother really was just a computer, as Jobs plainly believed.

"How are we going to get on the ship?" Violet wondered.

Jobs shrugged. "I don't know that we are, Miss Blake. It may not pass close enough."

"You don't think it's being sent to us?"

Jobs shrugged. "Whoever or whatever Mother is, and I basically think Four Sacred Streams told the truth and she's a computer in need of repair, she's way over my head. I don't know what she's doing."

"There are small boats on the ship," Mo'Steel called down. Then he shinnied down. He looked at his raw hands with interest. "Must've lost my calluses while we were in hibernation."

Wylson and Yago pushed closer. There was plenty of room on the platform, but the people still stayed close together for warmth.

"So? What's your report?" Wylson demanded in the all-business voice her daughter intensely disliked.

Mo'Steel hid a smile. "Seems to be coming this way. I didn't see anyone. But there are small boats, lifeboats —"

"Captain's barge," Shy Hwang interrupted. "A launch, a jolly boat, the Captain's barge, maybe more boats."

"Okay," Wylson said dubiously.

"If we could get a couple of us, maybe four or five would be better, over on the ship we could maybe launch one of the small boats, use it to ferry people over," Mo'Steel explained.

Wylson nodded. "We should send our strongest swimmers." She nodded at Mo'Steel. "You, of course. 2Face. Yago."

Yago snorted. "I'm not jumping back in that water. It's freezing."

"You're a strong swimmer."

"I'm needed here," Yago said without elaborating.

Violet's mother hesitated, like she was going to argue, then let it go with a petulant sigh.

"Tamara? One of us could hold the baby."

"I'll go," Tate said quickly. "Tamara has the baby to think about. I'll go instead."

Tamara didn't bother to respond, just looked bored and indifferent.

Violet frowned. That was not the first time that Tate had seemed solicitous of Tamara. Was Tate trying to curry favor with Tamara?

"I can go," Jobs said.

Mo'Steel shook his head. "No, man. You stayed too long in the drink the last go-round. You've paid your dues. Besides, you're not all that great in the water."

Jobs didn't argue. He seemed to accept his friend's judgment. *They had an interesting relationship,* Violet thought. In anything intellectual Mo'Steel deferred happily to Jobs, and in anything physically challenging Jobs did the same in reverse. Instead of a friendship based on shared interests they had a friendship based on entirely separate territories. The only thing they had in common was that they liked each other.

It made Violet a little jealous. It occurred to her suddenly that she had formed no attachments to anyone here, not really. She should be close to her mother, but that was hopeless. 2Face was the right age and gender, but 2Face was much more like Wylson — they should be mother and daughter. Or father and son, she added dryly.

Tate? Well, Violet hadn't really spent any time with Tate, didn't really know her.

"I'll go," Violet said, surprising herself as well as everyone else.

"That silly dress nearly drowned you the last time," Wylson snapped.

"Yes, I know, Mother, I should be dressed like a man," Violet muttered. She slipped out of her dress, not an easy thing since it was sopping wet. She was rewarded with the sight of Jobs staring fixedly out at the water and a horrified Mo'Steel blushing bright red.

"Oh, for crying out loud, Mo, it's no different than a two-piece bathing suit," Violet said.

"Uh-huh," he said in a strangled voice.

Wylson sent her daughter a doubtful look, like she wasn't quite sure whether she was proud or concerned. Violet gave her nothing back.

"Okay, then," Wylson announced, "It's Mo'Steel, 2Face, Tate, and Dallas."

"My name is Violet," she grated.

"Anyone know how to stop that ship and launch the boats?" Burroway wondered.

"Didn't anyone read C.S. Forester or Patrick O'Brian?" Olga asked.

"Every word," Shy Hwang said with a grin. "I know the names of everything. But I have no idea how to do anything."

"It's a machine," Jobs said, head cocked, gazing

thoughtfully at the approaching ship. "It's a beautiful machine, but it's just a machine."

Mo'Steel frowned. "Yeah. Yeah. You know, maybe you should come with us, Duck. All those ropes and stuff . . ."

"I'll try not to drown," Jobs said.

The ship drew closer, slowly, slowly but inexorably. It was tilted over in the breeze, sails filled, ropes drawn taut supporting the three masts, rows of gun ports closed. It would not hit the *Dancer*. But neither would it conveniently come to a stop alongside *David* and allow everyone to simply hop aboard.

"I guess we better get going. We have to get in front of it," Mo'Steel said.

Violet stared at the expanse of water and remembered the paralyzing chill. If they didn't get aboard the ship, they would drown before they could get back.

Stupid to volunteer? Probably.

"Bye," Violet said, not looking at her mother specifically.

"Good luck, honey."

CHAPTER SEVENTEEN

"WE NEED TO SLOW THIS BIG GIRL DOWN."

It was not easy.

Twenty minutes' hard swim, full tilt, the five of them going on sheer adrenaline. Then, waiting, treading water, exhausting themselves while the ship bore down on them.

It had seemed to barely move relative to *David*'s pedestal. But down here in the water it was like a tanker going by, high-walled, dark-hulled, crashing and wallowing through the waves.

2Face waited with the others, worried by the way Jobs's eyes kept rolling up in his head like he was about to fall asleep and by the eerie purple of Violet's lips. *Violet had violet lips,* 2Face thought and didn't find it at all funny.

She was annoyed by Yago's chattering complaints, and more annoyed by the fact that he really was a strong, competent swimmer, seemingly tireless.

2Face prided herself on her strength in the water. She was willing to admit Mo'Steel to equal status, but not Yago.

There were, however, better things to worry about. Especially the fact that she couldn't seem to keep the feeling in her fingers.

The ship had three masts and a very long bowsprit pointing up and ahead, like a unicorn's horn. A massive anchor hung, well-secured by cables and pulleys, from the left side, the port side of the bow. That was going to be her way in. If she could grab it without being run down. If she could grab it with numb fingers and haul herself up on the anchor's flukes and hold on as the ship continued to smash its way through the waves.

It meant treading water right in front of the ship. Like standing on a train track and hoping to hop aboard the onrushing train before it killed you.

"Mo," she chattered. "Why don't you and Violet try one side and Yago and Jobs try the other?" She didn't want to split Jobs and Mo'Steel up, but Violet seemed to be in slightly worse shape than Jobs now, and she could count on Mo'Steel to try to save her.

No one argued. No one was all that anxious to take her chosen position away from her. If she missed, she'd be run down by the ship.

They began to drift away in opposite directions, staying close enough to the path of the ship, they hoped, to grab onto a rope or whatever, and just far enough out to avoid being run down.

2Face waited alone. The ship came on.

Countdown.

Closer.

It was massive, huge, a gold-highlighted behemoth. And it was so, so much faster down here, right under the bow.

2Face judged her moment, turned, and began to swim away from the ship. It was chasing her as she tried to match speed. The bow wave caught her and she rode it, arms windmilling wildly. The bow would crash through a wave and for a moment be exposed all the way down to the copper sheathing, then bottom out in the trough and nearly bury the anchor, before bobbing up to smash the next wave.

2Face tried to time it but her brain was in slow motion. All the energy she had went into her limbs as she fought to gain speed.

Then, all at once, she was under the water, swirling. A solid wall hit her so hard she bounced. Then it hit her again. The air was knocked from her lungs. She swallowed seawater and flailed madly. Her arms bruised against the rough oak of the anchor's stock. She grabbed on and now the bow was rising, rising, and up she went, up into the sunlight.

A massive rope cable led from the anchor through a round hole into the interior of the ship. Could she squeeze through that hawsehole?

The wave caught her off guard and nearly plucked her off her perch. She was plunged underwater, held down there till her lungs were screaming.

Then the elevator ride up and she could breathe. Breathed and scrambled, hand over hand, legs wrapped around the wire-brush texture of the massive rope cable. The hawsehole was just ahead.

Breathe!

Under the water, down and down, and all the while pushed and pummeled against the timbers of the bow, then up and up and move, move, move!

Head into the hawsehole. Too tight. No, she'd heard somewhere if you can get your head in a hole you can get all of you through.

She was halfway in when the next wave shot her through like a champagne cork. She landed hard on a wooden grate. The water sluiced around her. She took one breath, two, then jumped up.

The interior of the ship was dark, almost totally.

She banged her toe into a bulkhead and instantly banged her head into a low timber.

No time to do anything more than curse, she moved as fast as she could, looking for anything that would lead upward. Stairs. She ran up them, oblivious to danger, her brain swimming, eyes unfocused.

Now, a broad staircase led up. Up she ran. Up again, past a hulking cannon.

She emerged on deck, outside, sunlight and air. The boats were there, but way too big on closer inspection to just gaily toss over the side.

Where were the others?

"2Face!"

It was Mo'Steel, just dragging himself up over the side.

"Mo!"

"Violet," he gasped. "Get a rope."

2Face searched, found a neatly coiled rope, grabbed an end, and followed Mo'Steel at a run toward the stern. They had to run up a short set of stairs to a new deck.

"Give me the rope," Mo'Steel yelled. He tied it quickly around his waist. "Wrap it around that cleat, it'll give you leverage. Bye!"

Mo'Steel leaped off the railing and dropped into

the sea. The water swept him back along the ship. Leaning over as far as she dared, 2Face saw Violet clinging desperately to a half-submerged gun port. The lid was slightly ajar and banging down on Violet's already damaged hands.

Mo'Steel wrapped an arm around her waist and pried her loose.

2Face was suddenly aware of Jobs and Yago standing beside her, drenched but unhurt.

"Grab on," she said harshly.

The three of them hauled on Mo'Steel and helped hand him and Violet up over the side.

Mo'Steel and Violet collapsed on the deck.

"Now what?" 2Face wondered.

"We need to slow this big girl down," Yago said. He alone seemed to have all his wits about him. Everyone else was exhausted.

"Step on the brake," 2Face muttered.

Jobs's eyes opened. He gazed stupidly up at the sails. Then down the length of the ropes. "The ropes there, the ones on pulleys? I think if we loosen them up, the sails will just kind of flap in the breeze. That'll be a start. Kill momentum first."

"Yeah, no problem," 2Face muttered. "There's, like, a million sails."

"No," Jobs said. "Not all the sails are up. Just the

ones on this forward mast and the one up on top of the middle mast."

Mo'Steel hauled himself up. "Let's get to it."

2Face saw *David* and all the anxious humans on the pedestal drift by. They waved. 2Face waved back.

It took half an hour to loosen the sails and slow the ship.

It took three hours of backbreaking labor to launch the smallest of the boats.

It took another hour of rowing to reach the *David*.

Night was falling by the time 2Face looked up and saw Burroway glaring down at her.

"It's about time!" Burroway snapped.

2Face was about to say something really, really cutting and clever, but she pitched facedown in the boat and did not wake up for many hours.

CHAPTER EIGHTEEN

"ANOTHER METAPHOR FOR LIFE."

The U.S.S. *Constitution*. Old Ironsides.

They'd found the name on the stern in gold letters. It was the fabled frigate of the early U.S. Navy.

There was no crew. There was food. Not good food, but food. And water. And wine.

Mother had done her research well. She had reconstituted the U.S.S. *Constitution* with every rope and sail and barrel of rancid salted beef. Just no crew. Why no crew? That was a mystery. Had Mother's sources been inadequate?

She'd surely used a painting for part of her source material, then perhaps a set of plans for the ship. Everything but people to steer and reef and swab the decks.

It was unnerving, but then, Jobs admitted, he'd seen crazier stuff since he'd awakened from the big five-century sleep.

The ship was just a machine. Definitely just a machine. That's what he had said before he'd seen it up close. Still, Jobs found it insanely hard to figure out. There were about a thousand ropes of differing diameters, all heading from the deck up to the stratosphere of sails. Ropes, sails, masts, yards, the rudder, they all worked together in some mysterious synthesis with the wind and the tide and the currents.

It was like trying to rub your tummy and pat your head at the same time. Times ten.

The ship should have had a crew of at least a hundred. It had a handful, and most of those were fairly useless. For running up and down the rigging, furling or unfurling sails, only Mo'Steel, 2Face, Roger Dodger, Edward, and Anamull were much use. Violet, Tate, D-Caf, and Billy were all willing, but not surefooted enough. Yago could be induced to help occasionally, but not often.

Tamara would have been the best, of course, but the Marine sergeant was concerned with carrying her baby and ignoring everyone else. As for the baby, it had developed a habit of following Billy Weir with what should have been its eyes. It made Jobs's flesh creep.

Olga would pitch in readily where she could.

Wylson would help out grudgingly, only after making it clear that she was in charge. The other adults, Shy Hwang, Burroway, and T. R., were basically useless, though Shy at least tried.

No one but Mo'Steel readily accepted Jobs's orders. Everything was questioned, everything disputed.

"Like trying to get a bunch of cats to drive a car," Jobs muttered.

Nevertheless, he was forming a serious affection for the *Constitution*. It was an amazingly complex but fundamentally logical problem, and he did love a complex problem. The ship rose and fell, rocked back and forth, creaked and leaked, and all of it was data. The sails filled or slackened, the ropes went taut or slack, and all of it was part of the logic problem.

Easy enough to run with the wind. But what if he needed to turn the ship? If he simply turned the rudder, the sails would turn as well till they lost the wind or were even reversed. Not like driving a car. The sails, too, had to be turned. There were long ropes that held the crossbeams, the yards, in a certain position. He could pull on the ropes and shift the position of the two sails currently deployed. Then the ship would lean way over, or begin pitching forward, or, if the rudder wasn't handled right, suddenly shoot up into the wind.

It was a logic problem and one of the most beautiful creations Jobs had ever beheld. The ship managed to combine Jobs's two great passions: poetry and problem-solving.

It was so cool.

It was just amazingly cool.

Jobs had managed to raise just enough sail to give the ship headway. He had posted Yago and T.R. to man the wheel — Yago liked the illusion of being in control. Olga and Burroway were down in the holds looking for food and water and anything else that might be useful. Shy claimed to be able to cook, so he was in the galley with Violet, doing what he could to produce an actual hot meal, the first in forever.

And up in the rigging, a hundred feet or so above the deck, Mo'Steel was playing like a young monkey in need of a tranquilizer. Edward and Roger Dodger were there, too, racing up and down the ropes, enjoying themselves.

Billy Weir stood with his back against a rail and looked up at them. Mo'Steel let loose a whoop of insane laughter and Billy smiled for the first time in Jobs's memory.

Violet appeared through a hatchway. She was carrying two mugs in her four-fingered hand, using the other hand to hold onto anything that would give her support.

"Hey," she said. "You drink coffee?"

"Never used to," Jobs admitted. "But I just started."

He took the cup. The smell caught him unprepared. In a flash he was home, back on Earth, back in Monterey in his kitchen and it was morning and his father was grumpy and his mother was asking everyone if they'd taken their vitamins and Edward was cranking the volume up on the TV, watching cartoons, and Jobs was pouring himself a big bowl of cereal and wondering if he'd forgotten to do any homework.

Jobs took a shaky breath.

Violet nodded. "It's the smell," she said. "It's very evocative."

Jobs nodded. "Yeah."

"It's probably not helpful to think of all the things we've lost. Coffee being just one. Chocolate. Ice-cold milk. Our dignity."

Jobs smiled. "You haven't lost your dignity, Miss Blake." He sipped the coffee. "It tastes like coffee. Mother must have re-created the chemical formula."

"She created beans. We had to grind them up. We're hoping Mother has some idea what beef tastes like, too. Mr. Hwang is cooking a stew."

"My God, is that coffee?" Olga moaned, approaching like a zombie chasing fresh meat.

"There's a whole big pot down in the galley," Violet said. "Just go down these steps and —"

"I'll follow the smell," Olga assured her.

Violet pointed with her mug. "That's Picasso's horse. It's in Chicago. The real one. I mean, it was. Back when there was a Chicago."

Jobs nodded. The statue was as big as all the weird statuary they'd passed through, more abstract than many, less creepy than the Sphinx they'd drifted past.

"This is really quite amazing," Violet said. "You realize that if we could control Mother, or at least communicate with Mother, she could create an absolute fantasy world for us. She could re-create Earth, I suppose. Or a version of it."

"Only with Riders and Blue Meanies," Jobs noted. "And maybe others, too. Yeah, it's an amazing ship. Hard to remember sometimes that's all it is, a ship. The illusion is so perfect."

"Can you steer this ship?"

He shrugged. "Steer it where? Wylson . . . I mean,

your mom, she hasn't exactly said where I should head."

"She doesn't know. And she can't admit she doesn't know. I guess no one knows." She shifted her gaze to look at Tamara and the baby. "Or at least, if someone knows, that someone isn't telling the rest of us."

Jobs nodded. "In answer to your question, no, I can't really steer. I mean, a little left, a little right, I can avoid running into the statues. But this ship should be able to move not just with the wind, but against the wind, or at an angle to the wind, anyway. I think I get the theory, but it would take a lot more people than we have. And if there's a storm . . . I'm worried about that. The wind is picking up again."

"Another metaphor for life," Violet said dryly. "We can steer, but only a little, and only until a storm blows. We're in partial control of a ship that is, itself, inside of a much larger ship over which we have no control. I wonder if Mother is some sort of philosophy teacher."

"Hey! Down on deck there! Ahoy!" Mo'Steel yelled down from the lofty heights.

"Ahoy," Jobs repeated with a wry look. "Ahoy back at you!" he yelled.

"Look up ahead, Duck," Mo'Steel yelled down. "There's some kind of statue, but it looks different."

"Okay," Jobs replied, not terribly interested.

"Hey, Jobs, man. I think there's Meanies flying all around it."

CHAPTER NINETEEN

"I THINK THAT'S COMING THIS WAY."

Wylson came up on deck in response to the shouts. Everyone was staring forward with an expression of concern. She noticed that Jobs was looking the other way, back.

Ahead, a statue like nothing Wylson had ever seen. It might have been a head of some sort, but nothing human, that was for sure. It seemed taller than the other eerie statues they'd passed. Taller, broader, in some way more solid and substantial. There was a sense of age to the object, a sense of age that had never been a feature of the other statues, even those meant to represent creations a thousand years old or older.

There was a battle going on around the statue. Blue Meanies, without a doubt. Their blue Mylar suits gleamed and flashed in the sunlight. Their hind legs glowed red where the rocket exhaust blazed.

They were engaged in a strange, balletic dogfight with smaller creatures that clung to the statue. They had multiple tentacle legs and Wylson could just make out a suggestion of liquid pink eyes. They looked like octopuses. No, squids, that was it.

The Meanies appeared to be trying to burn the squids off like jungle trekkers burning off leeches, using their maneuvering rockets to fry the creatures.

The Squid fought back with sudden jets that seemed to liquefy the rock of the statue and send it shooting out, like liquid fists.

Wylson was about to snap out orders when she remembered Jobs. He was theoretically directing the working of the ship. And he was still staring aft.

"What are you doing?" she demanded, annoyed.

"I think that's coming this way."

Wylson squinted. A dark cloud. Then, a stab of lightning within the cloud.

"What should . . ." Wylson started to say, then stopped herself. No questions, orders. She had to give orders. "Prepare for it."

Jobs's eyebrow shot up. "I have a crew of about six effective people," Jobs said. "And by the way, I'm not John Paul Jones here."

The cloud was clearly racing toward them now,

and at incredible speed. A cold breeze, like a fore-warning, dropped the temperature by twenty degrees in a heartbeat. "Lower all the sails," Wylson ordered decisively.

"No, I don't think so," Jobs said. "Sails are our engines. We need some movement to be able to steer."

"And you *know* this?"

"I don't *know* anything!" Jobs cried.

"You're guessing."

The boy took a deep breath and yelled up to the sky. "Mo! Furl all the sails on the foremast. Leave that one up on the mainmast. But try and strengthen it somehow. Do it fast! Yago! You make sure you have a grip on the wheel."

"You'd better be right," Wylson warned. She returned her attention to the strange battle ahead, secretly relieved to have Jobs to blame for any mishaps with navigation.

The battle seemed more important, anyway. She strode forward. A sudden shivering of the hull almost made her lose her footing.

"Opinions? Observations?" she demanded.

Shy Hwang shrugged. "It's the Meanies, for sure. I don't know what those other things are. They look like . . ."

"Squids," Wylson supplied. "Well, it's not our battle. We'd better steer away. Jobs!" she yelled back to him.

No answer. Irritated, she turned and froze.

The cloud was a black wall crackling with electricity. The sun still shone, illuminating Jobs, the white sails above, the gleaming wooden deck.

And then, in a heartbeat, the storm hit.

The wind picked Wylson up and drove her forward. She grabbed a railing and held on. The entire ship heeled wildly over, over, over, as if it would capsize. There was a terrible rending sound and screams and a wall of water crashed down over Wylson.

She felt her fingers slipping. Felt her body become weightless, lifted up, carried head over heels, swept away, fingers grabbing onto nothing, no air, sucking water into her lungs, and then, all at once, she knew she was no longer on the ship.

Jobs was on his face, clutching desperately to a wooden grate. The deck was as pitched as a roof. Water rolled across him, loosening his hold, filling his mouth. He ducked his head down and the water beat down on his neck and the back of his head.

The ship was going to capsize. It was going over. It was going to roll right over.

The whole thing was a logic problem, that's all it was, basic geometry, right? If the ship rose, if it came back up, if it didn't capsize, then it was geometry. Otherwise it was the end.

He saw it clearly, saw the way to respond, if only he lived that long. If Mo'Steel was somehow still alive. If Yago was still at the wheel.

If the ship rolled back up. If it didn't capsize.

Mo'Steel, with Anamull and Roger Dodger right behind, had raced from the mainmast to the foremast. Easy enough in theory. There was a thick rope leading from the mainmast's top platform, two-thirds of the way up, down at an angle to the foremast's platform — what Shy Hwang called "a top."

The movement involved pain. The rope was rough and ripped flesh from already raw hands. Mo'Steel left his own blood on the rope but he and the rest could all see the peril approaching.

Edward and 2Face had gone in the other direction, climbing up the mainmast to reach the topsail. Jobs had said to strengthen that sail. How they were to do that Mo'Steel didn't know. But he did know they needed less sail when the storm hit, that was fairly obvious.

Two sails were drawing on the foremast. Mo'Steel raced out along the yard, the horizontal beam that supported the sail itself, ready to begin grabbing up handfuls of canvas and furl the sail, when time ran out.

The storm hit and Mo'Steel held on by wrapping his body over and around the yard.

The ship heeled over and all of a sudden it wasn't the deck below him but the sea. The deck of the ship was pitched sharply and covered in green foam.

"No way she's coming up, no way," Mo'Steel muttered, readying himself to be plunged into the water.

In a flash of lightning he saw a face in the sea below him. Wylson! She was choking, staring up to heaven, then she was under, gone.

The ship began to rise, slowly, painfully slowly, she righted.

Mo'Steel saw Jobs. Saw Violet. Both holding on. He tried to look for the other mast monkeys, but the sails had been ripped from their bindings and now hundreds of square yards of wet canvas were whipping everywhere.

Lightning struck the mizzenmast with a terrify-ingly loud crack. And in the flash Mo'Steel saw Tamara, moving with superhuman speed, running across the still-angled deck. She ran straight for Billy Weir, grabbed him up bodily, and threw him over the railing into the sea.

Without thinking, Mo'Steel gathered his legs up under him and leaped as far as he could. He fell through driving rain and hit the water.

CHAPTER TWENTY

"IF WE'RE GOING INTO A BATTLE, I WANT TO BE ABLE TO SHOOT BACK."

The *Constitution* rose.

The sails were gone, all but a scrap hanging from the top of the mainmast.

Jobs could barely breathe for the rain that came down like a waterfall.

He staggered back to the wheel. Yago was there, but down on hands and knees, winded. Jobs grabbed him by the shirt and hauled him up.

The two of them grabbed the wheel. The wheel spun, throwing Jobs aside. Up and at it again, they grabbed the fast-spinning spokes and Jobs felt as if his arms would be yanked out of his shoulders.

T.R., sliding past on a sheet of foam. The psychiatrist hit something solid and stuck.

"T.R.! Help us!" Jobs yelled, screaming to be heard over the howl of the wind.

The three of them managed to hold the wheel. "Run with the wind!" Jobs shouted. "Steer straight."

"We'll run right into the battle!" Yago screamed back, his face inches from Jobs.

"No choice!"

The wind's violence declined by a few degrees, but the wheel continued to fight them, shoving the three of them one way or the other.

Jobs spared a moment to look up at the masts. He spotted Edward holding on for dear life. He didn't see Mo'Steel, but the flapping sails and whipping ropes obscured everything.

Ahead, the battle of the Meanies and the Squids raged, only intensified by the squall that now passed around them, smashing careless Meanies together.

"Ten minutes, we'll be there," Jobs said.

"We have to turn around," Yago said.

"No sails, Yago. We don't have an engine, all we have are sails, and all that's moving us now is the current and the pressure of the wind on the masts and rigging. If we're lucky we can just scrape past the statue."

Violet came running up. Her blond hair streamed out behind her, pulling her features back like a bad facelift. "My mom's overboard! I saw her get swept over. We have to do something."

Jobs shook his head. "Miss Blake, we can't do anything."

"But she'll drown!"

Jobs shook his head again, emphatically, not wanting to think about Wylson or where Mo'Steel might be, or whether Edward would be able to get down from his precarious perch on the mast.

2Face dropped to the deck from above, rolled, and jumped up. "Jobs! Mo jumped! He jumped into the water. I think he was going after Billy."

"Billy?" Jobs looked around frantically. Wylson, Billy, and Mo, all of them overboard? He felt like he was back in the water, drowning. Too much all at once.

"Tamara did it. She threw him over."

Yago cursed. "If Wylson's gone, I'm in charge," he said.

"We're heading right into that battle," Shy yelled.

The rain slackened and the wind fell from a furious howl to a low moan. The squall was past as quickly as it hit, but the wind still blew, rain still fell, and Shy was still right: The battle was unavoidable now.

"We need to turn around," Yago said decisively. "Jobs, turn us around."

"You and Wylson!" Jobs snapped back. "You

don't get it: We're a sailing ship without a crew. We go where the wind blows."

Yago looked lost for a moment and Jobs would have liked to savor it, but his head was still too full of competing scenarios for rescuing Mo'Steel or alternately accepting that completely unacceptable death.

"If we're going through that battle, let's go through as fast as we can," 2Face said.

"That's right." Jobs grabbed at the idea. "Okay, we need more sail. Once we're past, if the weather calms down we can launch a boat and go back for the people who went overboard."

"Anyone who went in the water is dead," Yago said harshly.

Jobs flinched but did not respond. "2Face, can you get any of the sails to draw?"

She nodded. "I still have Anamull, Edward, and Roger Dodger up there. Tate? Dad? I could use both of you, too."

Shy nodded reluctantly.

"Okay, do what you can," Jobs said, grateful for her decisiveness. "But let me have Anamull. Send him down, I need someone strong."

2Face leaped back into the rigging and disappeared behind flapping canvas.

"Olga!" Jobs yelled. "T.R., Burroway, you, too. Yago, you stay on the wheel, hold her steady to pass just to starboard of that statue."

"What are you up to, Jobs?"

"If we're going into a battle, I want to be able to shoot back."

He turned to the nearest cannon. It was black-painted, maybe ten feet long. A huge iron cylinder mounted on a crude-looking four-wheeled cart. It was held snug against the side of the ship by ropes and pulleys. The wheels were imprisoned by chocks.

"We'll never be able to handle more than one at a time," Jobs said. "Okay, we're going to figure out how to shoot this thing. First things first. Olga? You've had a chance to look around this ship. There should be a special room with nothing in it but gun-powder."

"Yes, it's like a little bank vault almost. Two doors and wet flannel hanging to keep out any spark. There were a bunch of small barrels and some can-vas bags, like little rolled-up sleeping bags."

"Cartridges. That's what we want. Take Bur-roway. Bring us back all the cartridges you can carry. Also, one each of any kind of tool you see around there. Keep the powder dry, and hurry!"

"There're cannonballs in that rack," Anamull pointed out.

"Yeah. Okay, look, I saw this Civil War reenact-ment thing once on a field trip," Jobs said. "I was, like, seven or whatever, but I think I know how it's done."

"Oh, great," Yago carped from back at the wheel. "Then it should be no problem."

Suddenly a Blue Meanie buzzed past. It looked like a scared cat all done up in blue Mylar. Twin ten-tacles waved from the sides of its face. Its eyes were blank sensors. Its rockets roared, though what they burned was a mystery. Jobs knew that the Meanies carried weapons in those blue suits — tiny explo-sive missiles and withering fléchette guns.

The alien seemed to be surveying the ship, no doubt wondering what it was doing there. Jobs had traveled for a while in the company of a Blue Meanie named Four Sacred Streams. He knew something of their abilities and weaknesses. He knew something, but only a little, of their goals. He was not under the illusion that the Meanies considered the human in-terlopers as friends. But perhaps they were not ene-mies, either.

Maybe, in fact, a well-aimed cannonball might convince the Meanies that the humans could be useful allies. And the humans could use allies.

He patted the cannon. If they hit a Squid . . .

The enemy of my enemy is my friend, wasn't that the saying? If Jobs could fire on the Squids, he might ensure the friendship of the Meanies, and if that happened, maybe they could help find Mo'Steel and the others.

He felt a slight acceleration as 2Face and her crew managed to tighten one of the loose sails.

Olga and Burroway appeared on deck, staggering under the weight of bamboo buckets hung from their necks with rope. Each carried three buckets. In each bucket was one cartridge.

"All right," Jobs said. "We may not be able to steer this thing, but we might be able to fight."

(CHAPTER TWENTY-ONE)

"WELL, MO, YOU PUSHED IT TOO FAR THIS TIME."

Billy Weir was surprised by the attack. It had occurred in a flash. Tamara, drawing on the power of the baby, had simply snatched him up and thrown him bodily overboard.

The crashing sea had done the rest. A wave had smashed him like a fist, driving him down in a swirl of foam.

He sank, arms and legs extended, faceup, amazed and confused and uncertain.

Why did the baby hate him? What *was* the baby? Why did it want him dead?

And always: Was any of this real?

Hadn't he experienced memories like this while burglarizing other minds in hibernation? Wasn't this like something that Anamull remembered from childhood? Or was it more like the suppressed memories T.R. hid way down deep inside?

The water smothered him and for a moment he was inside Yago's claustrophobia. Of course, with Yago it hadn't been water, it had been the hole in the backyard and the collapsing walls of mud.

This was water. Unlike any other memory or imagined memory. Yes, it was different. And there had been the attack, that was true, wasn't it?

He saw Wylson in the water, too. He had been inside her mind, of course, or thought he had. Surely he remembered things about her that only she should know.

He saw her drowning now. She was barely moving. Maybe not moving at all, maybe it was just the water pushing her limbs.

Of course, Billy realized, *I'm not moving, either, and I'm not dead. Not yet.*

Should I be?

He hit a bump. The seabed? So soon?

He twisted around and his hands smoothed gray steel.

This was interesting. So much was new and interesting. Better to live.

He thought for a moment, and a bubble of air began to grow around him, a sphere in which he stood up, feet planted firmly on an artificial ocean floor.

Mo'Steel hit the water and plunged deep. Almost too deep. The water couldn't be much more than twenty feet deep.

The ocean had a steel floor. He saw the keel of the *Constitution*: It could almost scrape the seabed.

Mo'Steel came up to vertical, mentally checked to see if he had enough air in his lungs, and searched in a careful circle, all around.

He spotted Billy Weir some distance away. He looked as if he was standing quite calmly on the ocean floor.

Wylson was floating a hundred yards off, suspended, neither sinking nor surfacing.

Mo'Steel began to swim toward her but he knew his air would run out before he could reach her. He began to rise, calculating his angle so as to continue toward Wylson even as he rose.

He broke the surface and sucked air and rain. A quick glance at the ship still heading for an apparent collision with the statue, a quick prayer for Jobs's safety, a second breath, and down he went again.

Wylson was nowhere in sight.

Mo'Steel swam straight down ten feet and looked again. No Wylson. Not where she had been, anyway.

He cursed himself for needing to breathe and

swam deeper, turning as he went, searching in every direction. No Wylson. No Billy.

He touched down on the steel floor, almost weightless. Where was Wylson? Where was Billy?

The light shifted, a sunbeam broke through the clouds, and there she was, dead or very near it, now settling facedown toward the bottom. She was still thirty feet away.

He couldn't possibly reach her in time. Could he? And still get to the surface before he passed out or gagged on a lungful of water?

"I'm not losing her again," he vowed and started toward her.

The distance was an optical illusion. She was farther away than he'd thought, and now his lungs burned and his ears buzzed and his eyesight filmed over red.

He could feel the strength draining away. His stroke became less and less efficient. His arms . . . legs . . . woozy, definitely woozy.

Well, Mo, he thought, *you pushed it too far this time.*

Surface. Only way out. Up. Only . . . only . . . why was he bumping into the ground? Oh, man. Turned around. Kick and miss. Rising slow.

Don't breathe, man.

Don't breathe.

He breathed. Sucked in hard. Sucked in air.

Again. Another breath.

There was an air bubble around his head, like a diver's helmet. His face and hair were wet, but there was air. Impossible. He breathed again and wondered if he was hallucinating. Was he already dead? Was that it?

No time for that kind of nonsense. He had to reach Wylson.

She was drifting along the ocean floor, facedown. Billy was moving toward her, moonwalking, taking big, giant, weightless steps.

The floor opened, like an eye winking open. Wylson was sucked down in a flash. It was as if the ocean floor had simply grown a mouth and snapped her up.

Mo'Steel shouted, "No!" But now it was Billy's turn. The boy was being drawn down the same hole, sucked toward it. He didn't seem to be resisting. And it occurred to Mo'Steel that he couldn't resist, either, or shouldn't. Wylson might still be alive, Billy surely was, and Mo'Steel couldn't abandon them.

He kicked off and bounded toward the hole.

A swift current grabbed him and down he plunged, down into darkness.

CHAPTER TWENTY-TWO

"YOU MEAN, LIKE CAVALRY COMING TO THE RESCUE?"

"What are we doing?" Shy Hwang asked, his voice straining as he heaved back on the rope and, with the others, brought the first cannon snug against the now-open port.

His daughter, hauling on the same rope, answered impatiently, "We're trying to get up enough speed to pass the statue quickly."

"But why load these cannons?"

"Jobs thinks . . . I mean, I think if we're going to wander through a battleground we'd better be able to shoot. Besides, the Meanies could be allies. Jobs and Violet did okay with that one Meanie back at the Tower of Babel. Maybe if we help them out they'll be grateful. Come on, next cannon."

"Do we really need more?" Olga wondered. She was mopping her brow, sweat streaming. She was anxious, and not about the battle zone ahead. Her son had dived off the mast, presumably to go after Billy and Wylson.

Jobs put a hand on her shoulder. "Ms. Gonzalez, you know Mo. He's unkillable."

Olga tried to smile and failed. Jobs hid his own despairing expression from her.

"Come on," 2Face said harshly. "Okay, D-Caf, release."

D-Caf unwrapped the ropes holding the second cannon's lashings.

"Okay, everyone together," 2Face called out, the willing cheerleader.

She, Jobs, Anamull, Olga, and Shy all pushed against the massive cannon while Burroway and D-Caf steadied the ropes against the roll of the ship. After some trial and error on the first cannon — trial and error that had come within inches of crushing Anamull — they'd learned to compensate for the ship's movement.

The cannon moved by inches. Back, and tighten the rope, back, and tighten.

"Okay, pull out the plug thing," 2Face said when the cannon was far enough back.

"By the way, it's called a tampion, I think," her father offered. "The plug in the end of the cannon, to keep the water out? Tampion."

"Whatever, Dad. Okay, we need our powder cartridge."

The canvas sack was shoved into the cannon's mouth. Anamull, wielding the long rod, shoved it all the way down inside. Wadding went in next, then the heavy cannonball was rolled down the cannon's barrel. Finally more wadding was rammed home.

All of this took time. Lots of time, and when 2Face looked up from helping to restore the cannon to position, she saw that they were riding right into the thick of battle.

The Blue Meanies continued to zoom and turn like slowed-down World War II fighter planes. They burned the Squids almost delicately, touching their jets to the creatures, which then would release their grip and fall into the sea.

The Squids fought back with punches of transmuted matter. Up close it was fascinating to watch. The Squids seemed able to draw the very stone of the statue up into themselves in liquid form, spit it out, and suck it back in. It was like watching bullfrogs snapping at flies. Mostly they missed, but when they hit a Blue Meanie the result was shattering.

"Why are the Meanies so careful?" 2Face wondered aloud. "They have fléchette guns. They have missiles." No one answered.

Something was definitely wrong about the scene. Something was too careful and deliberate in the way the Blue Meanies fought.

"Okay, we can do one more cannon," 2Face said. "Let's go!"

Everyone groaned, but the groans were insincere. The battle was around them now, very close. The ship was ghosting forward, a weird intruder in a weird scene.

"Okay, haul it in," 2Face directed.

"Can we elevate the cannon enough to hit that bunch of squids there?" Jobs wondered aloud as he shoved and heaved. "We'll be there, in line, in two minutes."

"It might earn us some big brownie points with the Meanies," 2Face said.

"You mean, like cavalry coming to the rescue?" D-Caf asked, then imitated a bugle call before retreating into embarrassed silence.

"Pull out the tampion," 2Face ordered, with a rueful nod to her father.

Shy Hwang snatched the plug out. Powder cartridge. Wadding. Ball. Wadding. Then everyone was hauling like mad to shove the tons of iron into position.

"How's the slow match, Burroway?" 2Face asked.

Burroway held up what looked like a knot of rope, smoldering on one end.

"Don't forget, if we do shoot, these babies will come flying back on the recoil," Shy warned.

The statue was so close now. The ship would pass it by, but it would be a close thing. *It was a strange study in contrast,* 2Face thought: *the vast yet delicate ship, moving on the breeze, and the solid, immovable stone mass.*

A Squid aimed and fired a jet of matter, narrowly missing a Blue Meanie.

And then, another Squid fired. Maybe it had been aiming at a Meanie, but the shot, the tongue of liquefied stone, hit the end of a mainmast yard. There was a startling crack, and the yard split down the middle.

"Okay, that's our excuse. Elevate the cannon," Jobs snapped.

No easy task. The cannon could only be raised by inserting levers and forcing it up, inch by strained inch.

"They'll come around in a few seconds, Burroway — are you ready?" Jobs asked.

"Are you all sure about this?" Olga asked.

"No," Jobs admitted.

Then, a voice from far above, Violet, up in the rigging. "Don't shoot! I think —"

But Jobs and 2Face both had already yelled, "Fire!"

Burroway touched the slow match to the grainy powder in the touch hole.

A flash, followed a split second later by an ear-numbing boom, and the cannon rolled back.

The black ball could be clearly seen flying. It arched toward a cluster of Squids clinging to a low ledge. It arched toward them, missed by a dozen yards, and smacked into the statue itself, sending stone splinters flying.

"Cannon two, fire!" Jobs yelled.

A second huge explosion, a second ball flying, smacking the unaffected face of the statue.

"Reload!" 2Face shouted. The explosions had an amazing effect on her. They had sent a thrill through her, top to bottom. She was galvanized, rushed, exalted. The sulfur smell of the powder was sweet.

It had the same effect on everyone. They'd suffered too long without being able to give anything back. A grin lit every face. Everyone jumped to reload the guns.

But the explosions had also had a galvanizing effect on the other combatants.

The Squids began to drop from the statue, drop straightaway into the sea.

And the Blue Meanies turned, formed up together, and like a flock of birds all in formation, they attacked the ship.

"What are they doing?" Shy asked.

The first burst of fléchette fire caught Shy Hwang. And there was no way for him to have survived.

(CHAPTER TWENTY-THREE)

"IF YOU CAN KEEP YOUR HEAD WHILE ALL THOSE ABOUT YOU ARE LOSING THEIRS . . ."

2Face screamed and screamed and the sound echoed in Jobs's head, melding with the whir of fléchettes and the huge bang of the cannon and the cries of fear and shock from all around.

In a heartbeat the battle had shifted. Now the attack was on the *Constitution*. The Meanies zoomed past, firing fléchettes that chewed the railings and decks and masts like steel-jawed termites. Ropes parted, sails whipped loose.

There was a blur of movement and Jobs saw Edward falling, falling from the main top and yelling, yelling. Jobs jerked forward, stretched his arms out to catch his little brother, but by sheer luck Edward snagged a trailing rope. He landed hard but not injured, aside from rope burns that bloodied his palms.

2Face was still screaming. A burst of fire from a Meanie's rockets burned a hole in one of the remaining sails. The sail was too wet to catch fire.

A burst of fléchettes chewed a hole in the deck right before Jobs's feet. He jumped back.

What to do? What to do?

Fire the remaining cannon? At what? They couldn't hit targets in the air.

Tamara ran past, a blur. She flung herself down a hatchway, the baby in her arms.

Tamara was running away! She had always fought the Riders, but in the face of this aerial attack from the Blue Meanies, she was diving for cover.

"Surrender!" Yago yelled as he cowered behind the ship's wheel.

Jobs frowned. What?

"Hands up!" Yago yelled. "Everyone, hands in the air. Hands in the air. Get away from the cannons, you idiots!"

2Face still screamed, screamed as if she'd never stop.

D-Caf threw up his hands. Burroway did the same.

"We surrender! We surrender!" Yago kept shouting.

Olga followed suit, hands in the air.

"Lie down, everyone down on deck, lie down, lie down," Yago bellowed. "Show them we give up. We give up."

The scream stopped abruptly. "We can't give up!" 2Face shrieked. Her scarred face was streaked with tears. There were strange, livid spots in the mottled flesh. The undamaged side of her face was a mask of rage.

"They'll sink the ship, you idiot," Yago snapped. He was on his face, spread-eagled on the deck. Others were following suit. One by one, then all together at once.

Jobs dropped to his knees, hesitated, then fell forward.

Only 2Face stood defiant.

The Blue Meanies drifted past, slowly, watching, mechanical eyes taking in the scene. The only sound was the muted roar from their maneuvering rockets.

Jobs knew the Meanies could finish the job in a few seconds. The humans were all exposed. The ship was entirely at the mercy of the aliens who called themselves the True Children of Mother.

Jobs hugged the deck and tried not to focus on the blood draining toward him.

The Meanies turned like a flight of sparrows, formed up, and vectored away, back toward the statue.

For a long time no one spoke, no one moved.

At last, 2Face snarled, "You can all get up off your bellies now."

Jobs rose, shaky, to see that the *Constitution* had drifted past the statue. It was 100 yards past the statue where the Blue Meanies now perched, unchallenged.

He moved to the larboard rail, stomach queasy, wanting to throw up. He stared back at the statue, took shaky breaths.

The Blue Meanies were moving into a circle now, flying in slow, sedate fashion around the statue while a group of six or seven stood atop the monument. Those standing waved their tentacles, synchronized, stylized.

Jobs was aware of Violet beside him. "Look," she said.

He nodded, not yet trusting his voice.

"It's something significant to them," Violet said. "I think it may have religious significance. I had the feeling . . . before . . ."

"It's just one of the statues," Jobs said. "It's just part of the environment."

"Maybe not," Violet said. "It means something to them. Watch them."

Jobs saw it now, too late. Realized now what Violet had figured out a split second before the fateful cannon fire. "That's why the Meanies didn't use fléchettes or missiles to scare off the Squids. They didn't want to hurt the statue."

"We hit it with a cannonball."

"Yeah."

Violet looked down at the water, now relatively peaceful. So much like a painting of a tranquil sea. "Do you think my mom . . . I guess it's possible she's not . . ."

Jobs wanted very much to cry and thought he might just do so. Mo was gone. Wylson, Violet's mother, gone. Billy Weir, that strange boy, gone. Shy Hwang gone.

"If Mo was here, I'd have him do the math," Jobs whispered.

"What?"

"How many dead. In how much time. How many left. How long before the rest of the human race is dead, too. Mo could do the math."

"Looks like I saved our butts," Yago said, striding up as cockily as ever.

"Surrender," 2Face spit the word at him. "Great plan, Yago."

"It worked, freak. We're alive. So how about, shut up, 2Face? Oh, and I'm sorry for your loss."

2Face looked like she might punch Yago. But then her fierce expression dulled and she looked down and away, and seemed to lose interest in everything but the distant horizon.

Yago smirked. "If you can keep your head while all those about you are losing theirs . . . that's a poem, isn't it? Right? Anyway, if you can keep your head while all about you are losing theirs, I guess you're the boss," Yago said contentedly.

"You want to be boss, Yago? Go right ahead. Boss of less and less," Jobs said. He felt sick and defeated. Beaten. If Mo'Steel was dead . . . *Clean sweep,* he thought bitterly, all except for Edward. Mom, Dad, Mo. Cordelia, back on Earth. The whole human race. A handful left alive, and that handful growing smaller and smaller.

Tamara reappeared on deck. Her eyeless baby surveyed the wreckage and grinned its toothy grin.

"A mess," Tamara commented without real concern.

"We'll fix it up," Yago said briskly.

Tamara cocked her head and laughed to herself. "So you're in charge now, Yago?"

"That's right," he said. "I am."

"Yeah? Are you in charge of *me*, Yago?"

Yago swallowed and did not answer. Tamara sauntered away with the baby on her hip.

CHAPTER TWENTY-FOUR

"ARE YOU STILL A HUMAN BEING, BILLY?"

The ground opened and swallowed Mo'Steel. The bubble around his head was swept away by a swift current. Down and around, like he was traveling through a corkscrew. Around and around, pitch-black, smooth pipe walls swiping his butt and back.

It was like the Pipe. Back before. The last really major rush he'd enjoyed on Earth, right before the end.

Yeah. That had been great. Of course, he'd had air back there.

Around and around and all at once he went flying, somersaulted, and landed hard and unprepared. He was faceup beneath a torrent of water. He rolled away and was facedown on a massively built grate.

The water sluiced around him, past him, then stopped.

Mo'Steel drew a few breaths, shallow and shaky. The light was dim and without obvious source, but was sufficient to see by. He was in a square room made all of black metal. The floor was a grate. Half a dozen pipes fed into the room, all dripping, none gushing anymore.

Billy Weir sat, stunned, in the corner. Wylson Lefkowitz-Blake lay dead, or very close to it.

Mo'Steel dearly wanted to rest but he levered himself up and went to Billy.

"You okay, Spacey?"

Billy blinked at him. "Tamara. She threw me overboard."

"Yeah."

"Where are we?"

Mo'Steel shrugged. "You got me. Down under that bogus ocean. Maybe it's —"

A metallic grinding noise, like a transmission in need of repair, interrupted his words. It stopped as suddenly as it started.

"Okay," Mo'Steel said guardedly. "I was going to say maybe this is some sort of garbage disposal system."

Billy nodded. "That makes sense." Then he smiled his tentative smile. "At least, I guess it does."

The grinding noise came again. This time it was followed by a snapping, electrical sound.

"We should probably get out of here, if we can," Mo'Steel said. "I hate to leave Wylson behind, though. But I guess we can't exactly bury her."

"She may not be dead."

Mo'Steel winced. "Man, I was afraid you were going to say that." He steeled himself for the inevitable, but Mo'Steel had a deep-seated dislike of dead things. The idea of having to take her pulse filled him with dread. He started toward her with reluctant, almost mincing steps.

Wylson stirred and Mo'Steel jumped. "Yah-ah!"

"I think I did that," Billy said, almost a whisper.

It took Mo'Steel a moment to consider that. "Say what?"

Wylson jerked back, up off her face. She did not move like a person reviving. She moved like a person who'd been yanked by invisible strings.

Wylson hopped up off her knees, stood as wobbly as a marionette. Her head lolled forward on her chest, but then it came up, too, and slowly her eyes opened.

She stared at nothing. She stared at nothing with nothing. The eyes did not track or focus.

Mo'Steel crossed himself. Then did it again for good measure. "What are you doing, Spacey Man?"

"I can bring her with us."

Mo'Steel heard a low, moaning sound and thought it came from his own throat. No, it was from outside. From beyond the featureless steel walls.

It sounded human. Maybe. Or not.

Again the snap of electricity.

"We need to get out of here," Mo'Steel repeated, unable to tear his eyes away from Wylson. She didn't breathe. The arteries in her throat did not pulse. Her eyes were dead.

"I don't see a door," Billy said.

"Yeah. Me, neither."

Neither spoke as the snap of electricity outside gave way to what was surely the murmur of human speech.

Mo'Steel looked hard at Billy Weir. "Man, if you can do that . . ." He nodded at Wylson. "If you can do that . . . what else can you do?"

Billy looked at him with dark, troubled eyes. "I don't know, Mo."

"Enough to scare Tamara and the baby," Mo'-Steel said. "Are you . . . are you still a human being, Billy?"

Billy shook his head very slightly. "I don't know what I am, Mo. I don't know."

K.A. APPLEGATE
REMNANTS™

Mutation

"THE MOST WE CAN DO IS OFFER A PRAYER."

Mo'Steel got up and started to yell. "Hello! Help! Whoever is out there, let us out of here!"

Billy Weir did not move. He could wait.

Billy felt dizzy, drunk with the sights and sounds flooding into his mind and with the reactions of his body — skin breaking out in a sweat and then cooling, heart beating faster and then more slowly, mind flitting from thought to thought like a kaleidoscope. Everything happening quickly, everything flowing together. No time to think, no time to sort real from unreal.

"Hang on!" came a voice from outside. An adult man, Billy thought. Not an American. His voice had too much music in it. "We're going to get you out."

The door opened off to one side and light flooded in.

Billy stayed in the shadows.

Mo'Steel leaped out of the door and then took a fast step back. "Whoa! he said, shaking his head in surprise.

Two people were at the door A man. And another person, an extraordinary person. A person who looked like an illustration from Billy's *Encyclopedia Britannica.*

Billy remembered sitting on the floor of Big Bill and Jessica's bedroom and discovering the illustrations of MAN and WOMAN in the heavy, leather-bound p-book dating back to Jessica's own childhood.

The figures were covered with layers of transparent pages. Turn the first filmy page and you removed MAN's skin and exposed all that was underneath.

This person standing before Billy looked like that illustration brought to life. Wherever his clothes left his flesh visible, his skin was transparent. Arms, neck, face, scalp.

Billy saw the muscles in the monster's face tighten as he narrowed his eyes. Billy examined the veins running over and under the muscles like tree roots, the packets of yellowish fat in the monster's cheeks, the smooth grayish muscles sweeping from his forehead up over his scalp, the vulnerable pulsing of his fat jugular vein.

This monster had never appeared in any of his dreams.

Unless this was a dream.

He had seen things during the war in Chechnya. Dead soldiers, Chechen and Russian both. Shattered, bleached white bones. Raw hamburger flesh. But nothing like this.

The monster saw Billy staring and gave him a hard look. His eyes were the green of late summer leaves. Burning. Undeniably human.

"I am Alberto DiSalvo and this — this is my son, Frederico." The man's voice was twisted with emotion. Not a good one. Pain? Fear?

"Kubrick," the monster said angrily.

"Hey, I remember you!" Mo'Steel said. He was talking to the man, but his eyes were drawn back to the monster over and over like a moth flitting toward a light. "I'm Mo'Steel. Remember? You were hitting the snooze button right around the time the worms showed up."

"I — I think I remember seeing you," Alberto said. "Then, then, we must have fallen asleep. When I woke up, we were in some sort of, um, laboratory."

Billy felt a shudder. Not in his body — in someone's mind. He caught a flash of something that could have been Alberto's memory or Kubrick's or both mixed. Nausea, the smell of blood, a dusty machine cutting Kubrick's skin off in ridiculous small patches, anger, a sense of satisfaction.

Yes, Kubrick savored his father's anguish. His father had always treated him as if he were damaged — and now he was.

Or not.

Billy couldn't be sure. Couldn't tell if he was making this up, telling himself fairy tales.

He watched Alberto pull Mo'Steel a few feet away. "We have to find whoever or whatever did this to my son," he whispered. "Can you help us?"

"I thought you'd never ask," Mo'Steel said. "Let's go. . . ."